The
AMAZING ADVENTURES of
ALBERT and HIS
FLYING MACHINE

The
AMAZING ADVENTURES of
ALBERT and HIS
FLYING MACHINE

BY THOMAS SANT

ILLUSTRATED BY DEE DEROSA

A Yearling Book

For my boys, who enjoy a good laugh

Published by
Dell Publishing
a division of
Bantam Doubleday Dell Publishing Group, Inc.
1540 Broadway
New York, New York 10036

JUVENILE
FICTION
SAN

No character in this book is intended to represent any actual person; all the incidents of the story are entirely fictional in nature.

Text copyright © 1990 by Thomas Sant
Illustrations copyright © 1990 by Dee deRosa

ISBN: 0-440-40814-8

Reprinted by arrangement with Penguin Books USA Inc., on behalf of Dutton Children's Books

Printed in the United States of America

July 1993

10 9 8 7 6 5 4 3 2 1

CWO

1

I was lying on my bed, relaxing, when the doorbell rang. It had been a tough day in the seventh grade, one of those days that makes you dread moving on to the eighth.

"Albert!" my mother called from her studio. "The doorbell rang. Would you answer it please?"

My mother is an artist and she spends a lot of time painting in her studio. Mostly she paints things like eggbeaters and pancake griddles and Tupperware. Lots of Tupperware. She says she's doing a series of paintings to capture the American kitchen. My dad once said that in some homes it didn't need capturing, that it hadn't escaped in the first place. All he got for that was a dirty look, though. On weekends, Mom loads her paintings in the VW bus and drives to shopping centers all over southern Ohio, to display them. She sold one last year, too. But what Mom really wants is to get out of the shopping centers and into the galleries. Just about anybody can exhibit at a shopping center, she says, but real artists exhibit at galleries.

So I rolled off the bed and shuffled downstairs and opened the front door. A mailman was standing there.

"Hi," he said. He was a young guy, wearing a regular mail carrier's uniform, but with combat boots and a pith helmet. He had a thin beard and dark glasses. He glanced at the letter in his hand. "I've got a certified letter for . . ." he lifted his sunglasses and peered at the envelope ". . . for Master Albert Halperin."

"That's me," I said.

"Yeah? That's great. Here—sign at the X, will you?" He shoved the envelope toward me.

I slapped at my pockets. "I don't have a pen," I said. "Just a second." I spun around and went into the kitchen—I wanted a minute to think. As I rummaged through the kitchen drawer I wondered about that certified letter. I'd seen the return address on it: "Baker, Gunnar, and Hart, Attorneys-at-Law," with a street address in Los Angeles. Why would some lawyers be writing to me? I thought maybe old man Kellogg was suing me for the time I drove a golf ball—accidentally of course—right through his front window and hit his cat. But I paid for the window, and the cat was eventually all right. It just acted dizzy for a few days. I shoved aside food coupons and twist ties for garbage bags and the warranty on the dishwasher. No, it wouldn't be old man Kellogg. Besides, he wouldn't hire lawyers from Los Angeles to sue me. He'd get somebody local, somebody from Cincinnati. I couldn't figure it out, so I finally grabbed an ink-smeared pen, traced a couple of swirls on a scrap of paper to see if it worked, and went back to the front door.

I signed the receipt, and the mailman tore off about six copies of the documentation pasted to the envelope and handed it to me. Staring at the envelope, I headed back upstairs.

"Albert?" my mom called. "Who was it?"

"Mailman," I said.

"Anything important?"

"No," I said, shoving the envelope into my back pocket. "Nothing important."

At least, I didn't think it was important then.

I went back in my room and flopped onto the bed. The old springs squeaked.

"Don't get your shoes on the bedspread, Albert," my mother called.

I shifted my feet slightly so they were dangling over the edge. Then I pulled the envelope out of my pocket and tore it open. My stomach felt fluttery. I knew something interesting was about to happen, but I didn't know if it would be good interesting or bad interesting.

I unfolded the letter. It was typed on fancy paper the color of whipping cream and as stiff as new money, and was dated three days earlier.

This is what the letter said:

Master Albert Halperin
1600 Rose Avenue
Carlyle, Ohio 45226

Dear Master Halperin:

As you are aware, your great-uncle, Albert Karl Halperin, passed away approximately six months ago. Since then, this law firm has been working to move his estate through the probate proceedings. We are writing to inform you that you are one of the beneficiaries of his estate. The terms of his will state: "Anybody who's named Albert Halperin who dies without leaving anything for somebody else named Albert Halperin to remember him by would be a blamed fool. And I ain't, so I won't." This firm is not certain it fully understands your late great-uncle's reasoning in this matter, but his judgment has been upheld in court.

Therefore, the attached cashier's check represents a full payment to you of your inheritance. May we wish you our sincere condolences on the passing of your great-uncle. Hoping we may serve you further in the future, we remain

Sincerely yours,

Morton K. Hart

Morton K. Hart
Attorney-at-Law

And attached to the letter was a cashier's check made out to me, Albert Halperin.

A check for one thousand dollars!

2

"You could put it in the bank and save it for college," my father said between bites of mashed potatoes.

I nodded and studied my food carefully.

"You could give it to me," my sister said.

"Ha! Fat chance of that," I explained in a nice tone of voice.

"You dummy!" my sister commented.

"That's enough, you two," my mother said for about the twelfth time during dinner.

"Well, gollee, Mom!" Greta wailed, wrapping herself around "gollee" like it had seventeen syllables. "I don't see why old uncle what's-his-face couldn't have left a thousand for me, too. Or given us both five hundred. It's not fair!" She clunked her fork down on her plate. Personally, I didn't think Greta could be trusted with sharp utensils yet.

"His name was Uncle Albert," I said proudly. "And maybe if your name was Albert, too, he would have left you a fortune. Tough luck!"

Uncle Albert was really my dad's uncle. He had been married, but his wife died a long time ago. I guess maybe because he didn't have any kids of his own, he took a bit more interest in me. Especially since I was named after him.

Greta made a face at me, but I didn't mind. She could keep her face. I had the money. And I could see that it was driving her crazy. My sister was fifteen and thought she was the uncrowned princess of the world. There was something wrong with Greta. Unfortunately, I was the only one who seemed to realize it. Mostly I just tried to ignore her, but that definitely wasn't easy—ignoring Gruesome Greta was like trying to ignore a rabid warthog loose in the lunchroom.

"Yes," said my father, "well, Uncle Albert always was rather eccentric. And you're a lucky young man. That thousand dollars will make a wonderful start toward your college expenses."

There was a longish pause. I had the feeling that I was supposed to pipe up and say, "Right-o, Dad—let's put it in the bank tomorrow and watch the interest grow!" Instead, I kept my mouth shut.

Finally, my mother said, "You do think it'd be wise to save it for college, don't you, Albert?"

Now she had pinned me down with a direct question. I wasn't sure what to do. Obviously, this called for a strategy.

"Well, that's a good idea, all right," I said. "The thing is, though, I want to be sure I use it so I'll get the most back for it."

My father nodded. "You mean you want to make the best possible investment? Very good thinking, Albert. Perhaps we can compare the interest rates at the various banks and even take a look at long-term investments."

"Yeah, but I was thinking of a slightly different kind of investment," I said.

Dad paused with a forkful of peas halfway home. He looked at me suspiciously. "You don't mean something like a certificate of deposit or money market fund, I suppose."

7

"No, Dad, I don't."

Greta butted in, "I'll bet it's one of your goofy schemes. Like the time you tried to sell mail-order peanut butter sandwiches."

"It is not!" I said, "and besides, that would have worked. People would have loved having a sandwich delivered to their home or office each day. How was I supposed to know the sandwiches would get stuck in the post office's machinery?"

"They were probably scraping peanut butter chunks off letters for weeks," Greta sniggered.

"Greta, please be quiet!" my mother said firmly.

"Yeah, be quiet!" I added, just as firmly.

My mother glared at me. "Now, Albert, would you explain your idea of an investment to us?"

"Well, it's kind of hard to explain. But I can show you. Wait a minute," I said, scrambling off my chair. "I'll be right back!"

I dashed upstairs to my room and began rummaging under the mattress of my bed. I pulled out a map of Hamilton County, a blue sock, an old apple core, some underwear, and a flashlight with a broken lens and leaky batteries. Finally I found what I was after: a copy of *Mechanix Monthly* magazine from the previous November. It was already turned to the right page and an ad in the lower left corner had been circled in red ink. It had been circled by me, four months earlier, when all I had was a dream without hope.

"Here it is!" I said as I ran back into the kitchen. "This is what I think would make a tremendous investment. And it would only use part of the money."

My father took the magazine from me and looked at

8

the ad. He rested his head wearily on his hand and sighed, then raised his eyes to my mother. He handed the magazine to her.

Greta leaned over Mom to look at it. She immediately began chortling. "I knew it! I was right—it is one of your crazy schemes!"

"What is it?" my mother asked. "A giant lawn mower?"

She looked at the ad again. It showed a machine about the size of a kitchen table. The lower portion was smooth and shiny and tapered very gently. The top portion was a motor and a bucket seat with some kind of controls. It looked like a cross between one of the bumper cars from the King's Island amusement park and a flying saucer.

"No, Mom! It's not a lawn mower. Look at the picture closely," I said.

She scrunched her eyes and peered at it even closer. But she just shrugged her shoulders.

"Don't you see?" I asked. "It's floating on air!"

The expression on her face changed, and my sister bent down to look at the picture once more.

"Why, Albert, it does look as though it were—"

"It's a trick," Greta hooted. "It's hanging there by an invisible wire or something."

"Here, let me see that again," Dad said. They handed it to him.

"It's not a trick," I explained. "It's really floating on air. And look at the price—only four hundred and ninety-five dollars!"

"Yes, Albert," Mom said. "But what on earth is it?"

"It's my investment, Mom." I turned to my father. He looked bewildered, too. "Gee, Dad," I said. "It's a Zephyr-car!"

The rest of the dinner didn't go too well. For one thing, my father failed to see how a Zephyrcar could possibly be considered an investment.

To me it seemed simple enough, so I tried to explain it to him. It all had to do with my morning paper route delivering the *Carlyle Courier* and the bike I rode.

My route went up Sycamore Hill Road—a mile and a half long and straight up the whole way. Going up that hill with a load of newspapers feels just like you're pedaling up a cliff. Especially on my bike. What a disaster! It weighed about five hundred pounds and was old, old, old. I'm not sure where it came from originally—the Wright Brothers probably built it. Considering how battered it was, I think it may have been used at one time by a Dutch Resistance fighter in World War II. My dad said it wasn't his, and my mother said it wasn't hers. Maybe it had been abandoned in our garage as a practical joke. All I know is that when I started delivering papers two years earlier, I asked for a bike and my mother said, "Why not use the one in the garage? It's a perfectly good bike." And that was that. A couple of new tires, a gallon of 3-in-1 oil, and I was riding a bike that was bigger, heavier, and older than I was.

Is it any wonder I dreaded hauling myself and my papers up Sycamore Hill Road on that old torture device? But what choice did I have? It would take too long to walk the route. The papers were dropped off at 5:45 in the morning and I had to be back home and ready to leave for school by 7:30. And obviously I couldn't change the route to avoid Sycamore Hill Road. I mean, what would I say to the subscribers? "Sorry, folks, you don't get to subscribe to a newspaper because your street's too steep?" And it wouldn't do any good to ride the route backward, because

then I'd have to go up Bennington Avenue—just as long, just as steep. My route was a loop that went up the bluffs along the river, circled around a few times, and then went downhill again. If you drew a map of it, it'd look like a noose—with me in the middle of it.

I could have bought a new bike, I suppose, although I didn't have enough money for one before Uncle Albert's donation arrived. And, to tell you the truth, I didn't want one anyway. I was twelve years old—too old for a bike and too young for a motorcycle.

But a Zephyrcar would be the perfect answer. If I had a Zephyrcar, I could deliver my papers each morning a little faster. And by delivering them faster, I could actually increase the route and make more money. I would have more time to devote to my studies and would be less tired. By devoting more time to my homework, I would get better grades. And then I would be able to get into college in the first place and use the rest of the money Uncle Albert left me, plus all the extra money I made from the paper route, to pay my tuition. It all seemed clear to me. I tried to help my parents see it. My father just shook his head and massaged his sinuses.

But my mother spoke up. "Absolutely not! This thing doesn't look safe."

"Oh, it's safe," I said. "They wouldn't be able to sell them if they weren't safe, would they? See, there's a big fan underneath it that generates lots of air and the whole thing lifts off the ground and floats. It's an air-cushioned car."

"And you're an air-cushioned creep," said Greta.

"Albert," Dad began in his let's-start-by-being-patient-and-see-where-that-gets-us voice, "I doubt that it would work and I doubt that it would be any kind of investment at all. It would be a waste of four hundred and ninety-five dollars plus shipping plus C.O.D. charges. That's more than half your money!"

"Yeah, but . . ."

"Let me look at this," he said, studying the magazine ad carefully. He read the description of the Zephyrcar and looked closely at the picture. He's an engineer and I figured he was looking at it for a reason.

Finally he said, "Albert, there's about one chance in a hundred that it'd ever get off the ground. I don't think it's been designed for sufficient stability, the engine looks too small, and it appears to be vented so that the exhaust goes right under the operator's seat."

On and on he went, explaining why it would never fly. What could I say? He's the engineer—a structural designer for Aerotech International. But I figured I knew a thing or two myself. Who had won the Carlyle Middle School science fair two years in a row? Me. Who had built his own rocket and successfully launched a mouse into space when he was only ten? Me. And I just knew the Zephyrcar would fly. After all, it was flying in the picture, wasn't it? But I also knew he'd already given me his answer: No way!

My mother took an apple pie out of the oven. It smelled delicious. While Dad was getting down the dessert plates, Greta cleared away the dirty dishes.

"Anyway," Greta sneered in her usual Godzilla-like manner, "if you did get one of those things you'd probably blow it up or fly it into a tree or dump it over the flood wall into the river."

She thought she was pretty funny and started chuckling to herself.

"No," I said. "I'd just land it on Bobby Herbert's car and make a convertible out of it, that's all. While you two were in it!"

Bobby Herbert was her boyfriend and she thought he was a big deal because he had a broken-down old Ford Galaxie that used to belong to his mother. Some car! Its engine sounded like a blender filled with rocks.

"You just try it," she said, "and see what Bobby does to you."

Mom put the apple pie on the table, and Dad passed out the plates and forks. "Who wants milk?" Greta asked. None of them seemed to care that Uncle Albert had left me a thousand dollars. I just sat there and watched them, and got madder and madder.

Finally I exploded.

"Well, I'll say one thing," I blurted to nobody in particular, "if I had a kid and his great-uncle left him a thousand bucks and that kid wanted to use part of the money in a perfectly good way to get something he knew he could really use, I wouldn't go saying he couldn't do it, even if I didn't think it was so great, because it's his money, so there!"

And with that powerful blast of logic I stormed out of the kitchen. Then I stuck my head back in and said, "And don't eat all of the apple pie, Greta. I still get to have some."

Later I came out of my room and snuck some pie. There was one piece left. It didn't taste as good as it would have hot. The apples were gummy and the sugar and cinnamon tasted sort of like glue. But I ate it anyway. It suited my mood.

I put my plate and fork in the sink and ran a trickle of water on them. Then I tiptoed out of the kitchen and started back down the hall to my room.

"Albert, could you join us for a minute, please?" my father called from the living room.

I went in and sat in the recliner chair.

"Your mother and I have been talking," he said. "And we've decided that if you really want to order that Zephyrcar, you can."

I couldn't believe my ears.

"I can?" I looked back and forth, from my mother to my father. She seemed doubtful and reluctant, but he was nodding.

"Yes," he said. "After all, it is your money from Uncle Albert."

"May he rest in an appropriate peace," my mother muttered between clenched teeth.

Dad ignored her. "But there have to be a couple of conditions to this deal before you get the final okay."

My buoyant balloon of hope sprang a leak. "Conditions?"

"First of all, you can't order it until I check out the manufacturer."

I started to protest, but he cut me off.

"It won't take long," he said. "I'll do it tomorrow morning. I'll call the chamber of commerce wherever this outfit is based and get their report. Okay?"

I nodded. I just hoped they wouldn't turn out to be a Mafia front organization or something.

"Secondly, if it looks like you're not going to be ripped off too badly—"

My mother snorted and looked away.

"—then you can order this thing on the condition that you take care of it. Pay all the bills for it. And use it responsibly. No dumb stunts and no letting your buddies mess around with it. With those blades roaring underneath it, somebody could lose a hand or a foot in a second. You realize that, don't you?"

"Yes. I realize it," I said. Actually, I hadn't given the

matter much thought. But I saw what he meant—the Zephyrcar was like a rotary lawn mower, only more so.

"All right," my father said. "I'll start checking in the morning."

"Right, Dad. And thanks a million you two! Just think, I'll be the first kid on the block with his own Zephyrcar!"

"Yes," my mother said bleakly. "Just think!"

Somehow I had the feeling she wasn't crazy about the idea.

3

As I went out to the garage to get my bike at five-thirty the next morning, I couldn't help thinking how different it would be to deliver papers in my Zephyrcar. I would just fly out of the garage and turn up Rose Avenue to Sixth Street, where they dumped my papers for me. Then I'd load them into some kind of basket on the Zephyrcar—I'd have to figure out that detail when the thing finally arrived—and glide along my route, tossing papers onto doorsteps with the greatest of ease.

For the moment, though, I had to wheel out my museum relic of a bike and hook the canvas bags over the handlebars, and then grunt and groan to get rolling. That bike weighed just slightly less than a full-grown water buffalo and was about as maneuverable. And the seat was hard and cold.

I waited for my papers at the corner of Sixth and Rose. In a few minutes I heard Morris, my route manager, coming. Morris was okay. He got there on time, gave me the right count, and didn't hassle me about getting a bunch of new subscriptions.

He pulled up and jumped out with the car still running. He jerked my bundle from the trunk and tossed it down for me.

"How's my main man this morning?" he said.

"Cold and tired of riding this old bike, Morris."

"You ain't planning on quitting are you, man? Good carriers are hard to get, you know. And you're a good one, Al."

"Oh, no, I won't quit, Morris. But I've got something planned. You'll see."

He nodded and smiled. "Okay," he called as he got back into the car, waved, and rumbled off.

I kneeled down by the bundle of papers. I felt kind of good inside about what he'd said. But I had to get moving if I was going to be done in time, so I folded each paper and slipped it into a plastic wrapper. The wrapper was protection against snow or rain or heavy dew. If the papers got soaked and were unreadable, my customers would get mad and call up to complain. Then my mom would have to call Morris and he'd have to drive out with another copy of the paper. So I used the plastic wrappers about three-fourths of the time.

Heading up Sixth I threw my papers with the unerring accuracy that had made me famous all over Carlyle. *Whizz, thunk!* Right on the Gordons' porch. *Whizz, thunk!* Right on the MacPhersons' porch. *Whizz, splat!* Right in the Cantanellis' bird bath. Oh well, nobody's perfect. As I went to retrieve the paper and toss it on their porch, I reflected that I could probably do even better from a Zephyrcar.

As I pedaled through an intersection I was nearly hit by a car.

"Hey," I yelled, "why don't you watch where . . ."

But then I saw who it was and shut up. Because I'd nearly been run down by the Carlyle police department. Carlyle has only one police car, and only two policemen. And one of them was part-time. The rest of the time he ran the baloney slicer and burger grinder at Mickelmeier's

Meats. His name was John Bannigore and he was the one who had nearly run me down.

I think they gave him the night shift in the hopes that he wouldn't cause too much damage then. Deputy Bannigore —or Baloney Jack, as he was usually called—was about twenty years old, sort of muscular from his days as a high school hotshot hero in basketball, and a little slow upstairs. The rumor was that the only reason they let him be a part-time policeman was so that the Carlyle police and firemen's athletic team would have a chance to win the Hamilton County Athletic Association's championship.

For some reason he didn't like me. It all started the previous fall. I was delivering papers as usual and he was prowling the streets of Carlyle, stamping out evil wherever it reared its ugly head. It just so happened that my old wreck blew a tire and I was stuck with only half my papers delivered. I thought maybe he could put my bike in the trunk and give me a lift home—I know Sheriff Panziker would have—but when I told him what the problem was he got really huffy.

"You flagged me down for a flat tire?" he demanded.

"Well, yeah," I admitted.

"Do you realize that I was on official police business? And that you interfered with my carrying out that assignment?"

I could hear rock and roll coming from the cruiser, so I didn't think his assignment could be all that darn official. But I just said, "Sorry."

Wheels were spinning inside Baloney Jack's head, though. His eyes narrowed in concentration as he tried to remember what he'd heard in police cadet school.

"You got a license for that vehicle?" he said.

"You mean a bicycle license? Uh, no, not exactly."

"You got any kind of proof of ownership for that vehicle?"

"Nah. We found it in the garage. Nobody knows where it—"

He yanked out a pad and pencil.

"You got any identification?" he demanded.

"Aw, c'mon, Jack . . ."

He stared at me viciously.

". . . I mean, Officer Bannigore. You know who I am. I'm Alb—"

"You come here," he ordered, grabbing me by the arm. He pushed me into the police car on the passenger's side. Then he got in behind the wheel, turned off the rock and roll, and turned on his police radio.

He said some code words and other stuff and then a gargly-sounding voice came on.

"This is the County Sheriff Vehicle Identification Unit. Go ahead."

"Uh, right," said Officer Bannigore. "I have a suspect here without identification operating a vehicle that's unlicensed and has no registration or ownership papers."

"Hoo-boy," said the gargle, "you got a live one, sounds like. All right, we'll run a make on it. Give us what you can and we'll run it through the computer. What make and model is the vehicle?"

Officer Bannigore leaned through the window, knocking his hat off in the process, and peered at my bike.

"I don't know," he said finally. "Hard to tell. Just a minute and I'll ask the suspect."

"You'll what?" the voice asked incredulously.

"What's the make of that vehicle?" Baloney Jack demanded.

"I don't know," I said. "Wait a sec. I'll go look." I hopped out and went over to the bike.

In the background I heard the deputy say, "Wait a minute. The suspect got out to check the vehicle."

I heard a lot of gargly-sounding shouting from the radio, but I couldn't understand any of it. Meanwhile, I bent down and looked at the frame of my old bike. There was a faded decal on the center post. In the weak light of dawn I could just barely read it: "Continental." I figured that was as close to the make as anything else, so I went back to tell Baloney Jack.

"It's a Continental," I said.

"He came back," he said into the mike, "just like I told you. He says it's a Continental."

"A Continental! And you didn't recognize it?" the gargly voice shouted.

"Well, it's an awfully old one."

"How old?" asked the voice. "You mean an antique? Like with old-fashioned spoked wheels and stuff?"

"Yeah. It's got spoked wheels," said Officer Bannigore, slightly perplexed. "But they've all got spoked wheels."

"Not lately they haven't," said the voice. "Like for the last forty-five years or so. Holy cow—what a cop you must be!"

The voice's last dig must have nettled Officer Bannigore, because he shot back, "Well, I've never seen any that didn't have spoked wheels. Hey, I happen to own a Schwinn that's only about six years old and it has spoked wheels."

After a long pause the gargly voice said, "Schwinn?"

"Yup, a blue Schwinn ten-speed that—"

"You mean to tell me," the gargle roared, "that you called in a computer check on a bicycle? Is that what you mean? Because if you do, you stupid . . ."

Officer Bannigore frantically tried to cover up the

speaker with his hands so I wouldn't hear what was pouring out of it. "Go on," he hissed at me. "Get out. And let this be a lesson to you."

And almost before I had tumbled out of the police cruiser, he zoomed away. The noise coming out of his windows wasn't rock and roll, either.

So, anyway, as I watched Officer Bannigore drive up the road on this particular morning, I was glad he hadn't hit me. He probably would have arrested me for obstructing justice. Or maybe he would have backed up, run me over, and then arrested me for littering the highway with my corpse.

I went back to delivering my papers and thinking about my Zephyrcar.

Three blocks up Sixth I turned onto Seminole Drive, then wound all through the housing district there. It was a housing development called Indian Acres, and all the streets in that neighborhood were named after Indian tribes. There was Comanche Court, Apache Place, Iroquois Avenue, Sioux Terrace. A lot of little, twisty streets where I had about half my deliveries. After I was done in that section, I turned from Navajo Nook onto Sycamore Hill Road. That's when my agony began.

Like I said, Sycamore Hill Road was the steepest grade in the city, probably in the county. I think they made the road by paving a cliff.

In the winter when it was snowy I had to walk the route because it was too slippery to ride my bike. Suddenly I realized something I'd never thought of before. A Zephyrcar would work just as well in winter as in summer, because it could glide over snow or ice or water. I'd be riding

on a cushion of air, and it wouldn't matter what was underneath me. They could spread the streets with raspberry Jell-O for all I'd care! The more I thought about it, the smarter it seemed to invest in a Zephyrcar.

I began the long, painful climb up Sycamore Hill Road. Less than halfway and my thighs were burning and my belly hurting. It became extremely difficult to keep the bike moving forward and to throw papers at the same time. Now my rhythm changed. With each toss I groaned. There weren't many complaints about my deliveries, but those who did complain usually lived on Sycamore Hill Road.

I didn't think it was really my fault. I was trying to pump up that hill and throw at the same time. They should have made it a decathlon event. It certainly would have separated the men from the boys. "Tell us, Mr. Jenner, what was the toughest event?" "Oh, the combination bicycle ride/newspaper toss on Sycamore Hill Road, of course. That's by far the most grueling."

Finally I reached the top of the hill. I paused a minute to catch my breath and wait for the numbness in my muscles to ease up. From the top of the hill I could look down on most of Carlyle. The town was still asleep, except for me and Officer Bannigore. And there was some doubt whether he was ever fully awake, so maybe it was just me. No, there was somebody else. I could see an old garbage truck prowling through the streets like some hungry, clumsy dinosaur. And of course the Ohio River never slept. It just flowed along, day and night, fair weather and foul. Carlyle was built right on its banks, sort of nestled into one of its bends. Ten or fifteen miles farther west was Cincinnati. I could just barely see its skyline in the faint dawn.

My heart had slowed way down to about two hundred beats a minute, so I took a deep breath and pushed off again. I turned down Ridgeway, then over to McCracken Drive, then a roller coaster ride down Bennington to Rose, and then home. On a good morning I could do the route in a little more than an hour, half of which was spent on the hill. I calculated that in a Zephyrcar I could probably do it in forty minutes or less.

Breakfast was almost ready when I got home. Greta had apparently already heard that I was going to get my Zephyrcar after all, because she looked even grouchier than usual when I walked in.

"Good morning!" I sang out. "It sure is a nice day! Weather like this makes a person want to go for a spin in the family Zephyrcar."

Mom ignored me, Dad looked up from his paper and smiled, and Greta snarled. All in all, I felt wonderful.

"Looks like spring is finally on its way," Dad said. "I think I'll call about having the front lawn reseeded."

He and my mother began talking about how much it might cost and what kind of grass seed to use and whether to have a nursery do it or to do it themselves. Finally they both paused at the same moment to sip their coffee and I leaped in.

"Dad, are you going to check on the company that makes Zephyrcars today?"

He pulled a slip of paper from his shirt pocket. "I was hoping to, if I have time. I have their name and phone number written down here. Let's see—it's the Future Perfect Manufacturing Company. In El Toro, California."

"Oh. Well, I was wondering how long it would be before you knew whether they're crooks or not."

"With any luck, I should know by the time I leave work today. A couple of days at the latest."

"So maybe I could even order it today?"

"Well . . . maybe," he said. He stole a glance at my mother. He seemed a little more reluctant this morning, but at least he was still willing to go through with it.

All day long at school I sat at my desk, but I wasn't in any of the classes. No, I was in the seat of my Zephyrcar. I was zipping along, delivering papers in record time. I just about decided I'd get two routes, since it would be so easy and take only half as long. In math class I began to doodle pictures of Zephyrcars on my math paper. Mr. Dugan thought I was drawing flying saucers and told me to stop.

When I got home I ran into the house and hollered, "Mom! Did Dad call yet? Did he find out about the Zephyrcar?"

"Hello, Albert," she called back, "and no, your father hasn't called yet."

I went into the kitchen and got an apple out of the refrigerator. While I was munching on it, the phone rang. I snatched it up. I knew it had to be Dad.

"What'd you find out?" I blurted. "Are they crooks or not? Are they murderers, con men, thieves?"

It was very quiet on the other end for a long time. Then a woman's voice said, "Uhm . . . hello? Is this the residence of Mrs. Elizabeth Halperin, the painter?" It was a cultured voice. The kind you'd occasionally hear wafting up from the private boxes at Music Hall.

"Yes, this is the place," I said. And then, because I wanted to be helpful and kind of make up for the way I'd blabbered into the receiver, I said, "In fact she's painting right now. She's painting a muffin pan."

There was another pause on her end. Then the woman said, "She's doing what?"

"She's painting a muffin pan. And some silverware and a cookie jar."

For the third time there was quiet at her end of the conversation. I felt I was holding up my part pretty well, but she seemed to be dropping out of it.

Finally she thought of something. "Young man," she said, very precisely, "I certainly don't have time for silliness or foolish jokes. Good-bye." And the receiver clicked in my ear.

I was still staring at the telephone when my mother came into the room.

"Who was that?" she asked.

"Don't know. Somebody who doesn't appreciate art, I guess."

Mom looked at me like she was measuring me for a suit. "Well, I'm expecting a very important call," she said, "so don't play games with the phone." Before I could protest my innocence, she walked out.

I'd barely eaten two more bites of my apple when the phone rang again.

"Uh-oh," I thought. "There's Mrs. Prune-tonsils again. And I'll bet she's the important call Mom's expecting. She'd better not hear that it's me or she'll hang up again."

So I decided to disguise my voice. I thought if I talked real low and gruff, she might think it was my father.

"Hello," I growled.

"Hello?" said a man's voice. "Who is this, please?"

I wondered: Is she disguising her voice, too, to catch me off guard? I decided I'd better play it cagey.

"Who is this?" I growled again.

"I asked first," said the man. "Albert, is that you?"

Suddenly I realized who was on the phone.

"Dad!" I yelled. "Did you find out about the company?"

"Yeah," he said, "but what is wrong with your voice? It sounds like you're growling or something."

"Must have been a bad connection, Dad. You sound kind of weird, too, like a prune or something. What'd you find out?"

"What do you mean, like a prune?"

"Dad! The company! What'd you find out about them?"

"All right, all right. Well, I'm not sure how happy I am about this, but apparently the Future Perfect Manufacturing Company is okay. I made some calls and everything checked out."

"You mean . . ."

"I mean," he said resignedly, "that you can order it."

Poor Dad. He must have felt like a firecracker had gone off in his ear. I whooped and yelled, threw the phone down on its cradle, then went stomping through the house, bounding around like a kangaroo, careening off the walls and furniture, rolling over on my back in the middle of the living room, waving my arms and legs in the air, yodeling like an Alpine cuckoo.

I figure I scored about a 9.9 in the men's floor exercise.

I was on my third circuit through the kitchen when the phone rang again. Dad! I hadn't said thank you or anything. But he'd understand. He knew how excited I was.

I snatched up the phone.

"Just think!" I yelled into it. "I'll be flying all over town in no time. Flying! Right off the ground! Can you believe it?"

There was a long pause. Then a woman with a familiar voice said, "Yes, young man, I find that I can believe it. Now, will you please tell me: Is this the Halperin residence? Or is it a home for the adolescent deranged?"

"Ma'am," I said, "right now—it's both."

4

The next morning, after delivering my papers, I filled out the order form. I double and triple checked it to make sure everything was right:

The
FUTURE PERFECT
Manufacturing Company

733 Jimson Road, El Toro, Calif. 92630   (714) 555-2360

Yes! I want to own my very own Zephyrcar, the vehicle of the future. Please rush my Zephyrcar to me at the following address:

Name _Albert Halperin_

Address _1600 Rose Avenue_   Tel. _(513) 555-2316_

City _Carlyle_   State _Ohio_   Zip _45226_

Only $495.⁰⁰ for the complete kit!

Please allow 3 to 6 weeks for delivery.

After a microscopic scrutiny had assured me that everything was all right—no blanks left blank, no words misspelled, nothing left to chance—I placed the order form reverently inside an addressed envelope. I licked and sealed the flap, then reinforced it with two pieces of tape, just to be safe. I put a stamp on it, then put another one on in case the first one happened to fall off.

I put the envelope in my pocket so that I could mail it myself on my way to school, and checked my pocket half a dozen times during breakfast and a dozen more while I walked to school. Finally, there I stood, in front of the mailbox, holding my precious envelope. I had decided to mail it myself so that I could savor the experience. And so that I could be sure the order actually got mailed. It wasn't that I didn't trust the rest of the family, but my mother certainly hadn't seemed too thrilled about the whole idea at breakfast and Greta had been her usual semireptilian self.

I pulled open the box. It made a metallic squawk. I placed my envelope in the mouth of the opening. Then, with the feeling that I was taking an enormous, momentous step in my life, one that would affect my whole future, I dropped it in and let the door clang shut.

Then I opened it again and checked, just to be safe. It was in there all right. Now all I had to do was wait.

The order blank had said to allow three to six weeks for delivery. I made it through the first week pretty well, but by the end of the second I was like a shoe box full of coiled springs, tied down with a bit of raggedy string. The slightest jolt—the sort that the Queen of Monster Island, alias Gruesome Greta, might cause, for example—and ZING! I'd burst into a frazzle all over the living room.

But nobody bothered me much, not even Greta. One evening Dad brought home a little present. It was a large, thin, rectangular book, covered with dull gray cloth. On the front was a red inscription: "Savings and Expense Ledger."

"It'll help you keep track of your money, all your expenses, and any income you might have. It'll help you see exactly where your money goes. Because Albert," he explained in an ominous tone, "there just may be more expense to owning a Zephyrcar than you anticipate. Gasoline, engine tune-ups, parts and tools, and who knows what else. And it'll give you a chance to learn something about managing your money."

Oh, so that's it, I thought. It would be a chance to learn one of those Lessons of Life. Well, if the ledger eased Dad's conscience about letting me buy the Zephyrcar, it was fine with me.

But the ledger didn't help the days pass any faster. I had mailed the order on March 9th. So I knew I couldn't even hope to see my Zephyrcar arrive before the 30th.

All in all, it was a lousy three weeks. There was rain nearly every day, even more than usual for spring. And it wasn't just mild rain, either. We had thunderstorms and tornado watches every few days, the kinds of storms that rip the leaves and branches out of the trees and blow old scraps of newspaper up against the garage door. All of that rain didn't exactly make the time skip by. By the 29th I felt like a hundred pounds of firecrackers on a two-inch fuse.

Finally, though, the 30th came. And went.

No delivery.

Ditto on the next six days.

But on April 6th, as I headed down Rose Avenue for home after school, I noticed a large truck in front of our house. I began pedaling my old relic as fast as I could. Maybe this was it!

As I got nearer, though, I could read the lettering on the

truck. It said: "Marco's Nursery and Garden Supply." And when I pulled into the driveway, I saw two men in work clothes standing on the porch, talking to my mother. Another man was sitting in the cab of the truck.

"We've finished the reseeding, Mrs. Halperin," one of the men was saying. "We'll spray the area with some liquid fertilizer and put in the stakes to keep people from trampling across your new grass, and that'll be that."

My mother nodded and asked him how long it would be before the grass shoots sprouted. About that time I squeezed past, mumbling, "Scuze me, hello, Mom," and went into my room.

I threw my books on the bed and flopped down next to them. I felt let down that the truck hadn't been there to deliver my Zephyrcar. I lay with my arms folded, staring at the ceiling. Then I turned on my transistor and listened to some music. But I didn't like that, either, so I decided to go watch the gardeners. Somehow watching somebody spray liquid fertilizer suited my mood better than anything else I could think of.

They were just finishing when another truck drove up.

A young guy with a sandy mustache and olive green uniform climbed out of the second truck. He carried a clipboard in one hand and was obviously studying the house numbers. He walked up the driveway and down the walk to the front porch, where I was sitting.

All of a sudden I began to feel twitchy inside.

"Hi," he said. "Is this the Halperin place?"

I nodded.

"Good. I've got a delivery for Mr. Albert Halperin."

My heart was pounding now.

"Th-th-that's me. I'm Alberin Halperin. I mean, Albert Halpert. No, no, I mean ..."

He looked at me, and then said, "Uh, is there an adult here?"

"Yeah," I said, leaping to my feet, "an adult. Good idea." I spun around and stuck my head in the door. "Mom!" I hollered. "Come quick! It's an emergency!"

I heard a muffled crash from the studio and the sound of running footsteps. She burst around the corner and sprinted down the entry hall toward me.

"What's the matter?" she asked anxiously. "Are you hurt? Is somebody else hurt?"

"No, it's not that kind of emergency, Mom," I said.

She slowed down suddenly, put her hands on her hips, and stared at me. Then she looked at the delivery man. Then back at me.

"Albert," she muttered, "this had better be good. I was just starting to get into that orange juice jug I've been having trouble with."

The delivery man's eyes grew wide. I could see his lips move, but no sound came out. He was staring at my mother intently. Finally, he said, "Uh, is there another adult at home?"

"No, there isn't," my mother snapped in a tone that would defrost an Eskimo's freezer. Her eyes were aflame. "What do you want?"

Now the delivery man was rattled. "Well, I've got a delivery for Mr. Albert Halibut and I need somebody to sign for it."

"It's not Halibut, it's Halperin," my mother interrupted, "and Albert knows how to write his name, and he has the money to pay you, so I don't know why you need me." With that she turned around, muttering, "Now I just hope I can get back into that orange juice jug again!" And she marched back to her studio.

I smiled at the delivery man. "She's an artist," I said.

"Sounds more like a circus act to me," he muttered. He held the clipboard and showed me where to sign, took the check I had ready for him, then glanced at the bill of lading.

"Good grief!" he exclaimed. "This shipment weighs over two hundred pounds! What'd you do, kid? Order yourself a set of encyclopedias with cereal box tops?"

I was getting a little tired of this delivery man's attitude, so I said, "No, it's a neighborhood-sized nuclear weapon. Try not to bump it when you carry it back to the garage, okay?"

His eyes popped again and this time his mouth dropped a little, too. Then he thought about it and said, "Sure, kid. A neighborhood nuke? Tell me another one."

"All right. It's not really a nuclear weapon. It's really a one-man Hovercraft that skims along on a cushion of air and I'm going to fly it around town when I deliver my newspapers."

He burst out laughing, then went down to his truck, laughing and repeating to himself, "A Hovercraft to deliver newspapers. Ha, ha, ha!"

He looked into the back of his truck, checked his freight list, and shouted up at me: "Hey, you've got five boxes of stuff here! You know that?"

"No," I said. "It should be just one big one."

"Says here five of 'em," he replied. "Where do you want 'em?"

"In the garage, I guess. But are you sure there are five boxes?"

He didn't bother answering. He just started carrying boxes back to the garage. All five boxes had the name "Future Perfect Manufacturing Company" stenciled on the side, along with arrows showing which end was up and other directions.

Finally, he staggered by with the last box, a wooden crate large enough to hold a console TV set.

"Ugh!" he groaned. "What've you got in here?"

"I don't know yet," I said, taking a crowbar down from the garage wall, "but it's sure not going to take me long to find out!"

Five boxes. Five unlabeled boxes piled in the garage.

I stood there looking at them and suddenly realized the enormity of the project I'd gotten myself into. I was going to have to assemble this thing!

When I'd ordered it, I figured it would come assembled, looking just the way it did in the ad. But thinking back on it, I remembered that it had said something on the bottom of the coupon about "the complete kit." "Kit" was obviously the key word.

I began to rip the boxes open with the crowbar. The first one I opened was the large, heavy one—the one that looked like it could contain a TV set. It contained an engine. A completely assembled engine. What a relief that was! The engine was a little larger than a lawn mower, but its design was different.

The other boxes contained a strange assortment of parts. There were panels of purple aluminum, the kind they use to make small airplanes. They were trapezoidal and the bottom edge, which was the longest, was rounded. There were aluminum struts, and a big thing that looked like a toboggan. There were two propellers and a shaft as thick as my arm, and about a dozen gears, pinions, and rings. There was a chair seat and a chair back, neither of which looked very comfortable. There was a long metal rod with a knob on the end that looked like an old-fashioned gearshift lever. There was a chain, two fan belts, and a plastic bag filled with what looked like five thousand nuts, washers, and bolts. And, finally, there was a set of instructions.

Perhaps set of instructions isn't the right way to put it. Actually, it was a bound volume about as thick as the Carlyle telephone book, filled with schematic drawings, cut-away views, diagrams, charts, tables, and—most of all—directions. Page after page of directions.

I sat down on the garage floor and looked at the heaps of metal and plastic around me and sighed. It would be quite a while before I was delivering newspapers in my Zephyrcar.

That night, at dinner, I asked my father for permission to use some of his tools. And for permission to work in the garage.

"Okay, but I don't want to end up parking my car on the street for the next three years while you tinker around in the garage," he said.

"Well, it won't take me three years, Dad. I think that by the end of this summer—"

"The end of summer! Listen, Albert, you can have three weeks. And then, no matter what, you'll have to move it out of the garage."

"But, Dad, where will I put it?"

"I've got a suggestion," Greta said.

I resisted the urge to decorate her face with my spinach. Instead, I just turned my attention to Dad.

"I don't want to tie up the garage," I said, "but I'm not sure I can finish it in three weeks."

"I doubt that you can finish it in three lifetimes," Greta said just loud enough to be heard.

"I can, too!" I exclaimed.

"Children," said my mother, "please don't spoil dinner for yourselves by getting sent to your rooms without it."

"Well, Mom," Greta whined, "he went and spent all that money on this dumb contraption and now it comes in a zillion pieces. And I'll bet anything that he'll never get it to work by himself. Dad'll have to do it for him! And then he'll strut around like he did it!"

But Greta had made me mad. So she thought I couldn't do it? Well, I'd show her! I'd put that thing together, all by myself, and I'd do it in three weeks or else.

So I said, "Three weeks? Okay, Dad. No problem." And then I concentrated on my dinner as intensely as I could. Not that the plate was very interesting. I just didn't want to look anybody in the face.

5

The next day was Saturday. I woke up so early there weren't even any cartoons on TV yet. I gulped down a glass of milk and three bagels with peanut butter on them, put on my sweatshirt, and went out to the garage. I looked at all the machinery piled on the floor and couldn't help thinking it looked like several piles of junk. Then I jumped on my bike and proceeded to deliver my papers in record time.

When I got back, everybody was still sleeping. I lifted the garage door again and just stared. Then I picked up the instruction book and looked at it.

Have you ever tried to read a book written in a foreign language? Sometimes you see a word that looks like an English word. But you have no idea whether it means the same thing. That's how I felt looking at that instruction manual. Sometimes I'd come across a word or phrase that looked familiar. But I wasn't sure it meant the same thing that it would mean in a regular book. For all I knew, I could have been looking at a Russian fairy tale or an Arabic cookbook.

I sat down on the garage floor and began to read. I went through that manual as carefully as I could, concentrating on every page, even if it didn't make any sense. I looked at

the diagrams and found each piece they pictured, then tried to visualize how the pieces would look when they were all assembled.

Page after page, section after section, I forced myself to go on. It was awful, yet fascinating in a way, because I knew it would eventually mean something to me. And it wasn't too much worse than reading some of the books we've had to read for English class.

Three and a half hours later I read the last page. I hadn't understood any of it exactly, and yet somehow I felt as though I had an overall idea of what to do. I got up, feeling stiff and woozy, and staggered back into the house.

By then everybody was up. My mother was in the kitchen.

"Why, Albert," she said, "I was wondering where you were."

"I was in the garage, Mom. Do we have any aspirin?"

She gave me a searching look. "Are you sick?"

"Not really, maybe a couple of aspirin would do the trick, Mom, okay?"

She went to the cupboard and got a couple of aspirin for me.

"I think I'll feel better in about three weeks," I muttered as I went back out. "Or else I'll feel a lot worse."

Back in the garage I picked up the instruction manual and began to read it again. I went through it just as I had the first time, page by page. But, surprisingly, this time it seemed to make a little more sense. And it went faster. I finished my second reading in the record time of two hours and forty-five minutes.

I was beginning to get excited. Maybe I'd be able to do it after all, I thought. Sure, why not? I was a pretty smart kid, I reasoned, and this kit was designed for people without any special mechanical know-how. It said so right in the introduction.

I bolted lunch down.

"Do you feel better, Albert?" my mother asked while we ate.

I nodded as I stuffed the last bite of hot dog in my mouth. "Lots better, Mom," I mumbled. And then I ran back out to the garage and was reading the instruction manual for the third time before anybody could even ask what I was doing.

Three weeks later my Zephyrcar was assembled. Don't ask me how I did it, because I don't remember. Large parts of those three weeks are just a blur of purple aluminum, incomprehensible instructions, and the cold concrete floor of the garage. I lost track of time, I forgot where I was, I became totally engrossed in assembling that monster. Soon I was even dreaming about it.

The instruction book said that assembly should take between ten and fifteen hours. I figure I spent over a hundred. Of course, it might have been closer to ten or fifteen if I had done everything right the first time. Instead, I found myself doing and undoing and redoing parts of that machine time after time.

It rained a lot during the whole three weeks, so I wasn't missing much. Once, a couple of my friends, Pat Salerno and Kevin Wright, came over to see what was happening. They were just knocking around and found me in the garage standing in the middle of a half-assembled Zephyrcar frame, trying to install the plenum chamber cover.

"Hey, what's that thing?" Pat asked.

I jumped, because I'd been concentrating so hard I hadn't heard them come in.

"Why don't you guys warn a person before you sneak up on him?" I asked.

"We didn't sneak up, Halperin," Kevin said, "and what is that thing, anyway?"

Suddenly I made a decision. It wasn't anything I'd thought about in advance. It just popped into my head right then.

I decided not to tell them what it was. I decided to keep it a secret until I knew it would work. So I didn't answer them. Instead, I said, "What thing?"

"That thing!" they both shouted, pointing at the pieces of my Hovercraft.

"Oh." I shrugged and looked around as though I hadn't really noticed it before.

"Looks like a washing machine," Kevin said. "Are you putting together a washing machine, Al?"

Before I could answer he turned to Pat and said, "He's putting together a washing machine. Can you believe it? What a dumb way to spend the weekend."

Eventually they got tired of watching me stand there and they could tell I wasn't in the mood to go anywhere with them, so they left.

But I stuck by my decision. I didn't tell anybody at school or in the neighborhood what I was doing. I figured it'd be better that way. If it didn't work, nobody would ever know, except for my family—which was bad enough, with Greta and all.

And I also figured out a way that I could make some money by keeping my Zephyrcar a secret until just the right moment. A lot of money—enough to buy gas for it for a month, maybe.

I would sell tickets to its launching. People drive hundreds of miles to watch the space shuttle take off and land. I figured the first flight of my Zephyrcar was at least that exciting. And I could even raffle off a free ride on it. People from all over Carlyle would be excited about that!

I began to see that thanks to my Zephyrcar I might not even need my paper route anymore. As I worked on it, tightening bolts and clamping hoses, my imagination ran away, and I pictured myself managing the Halperin Hovertaxi Company of Carlyle, Ohio. Soon I'd have a whole fleet of Zephyrcars, maybe even buses and a ferry or two, to cross the Ohio. The possibilities seemed endless. I pictured my ledger filling up with entries on the income side and my savings account swelling with deposits.

So I was pretty excited when I tightened the last bolt and stood back to look at my finished Zephyrcar. It seemed to me that I'd done a pretty fair job of assembling it. Somehow I had about a dozen bolts and one short strut left over. And I had sort of scrunched one of the purple panels to get it to fit, but it didn't look too bad.

Now was the moment. Would it work? Had I put it together correctly?

I approached my beautiful Zephyrcar and patted it affectionately. We'd been through a lot together out in the garage during the past three weeks. But now the historic moment had arrived.

The engine had a rope-pull starter, like a lawn mower or motorboat engine. I grasped the rope, planted my foot firmly, and yanked.

Nothing happened.

Oh no, I thought. What have I done wrong? I'd followed those lousy directions so carefully! I picked up the instruction manual from the garage floor and flipped through it. It

was greasy and tattered and smudged. Was there some secret locked in its pages that I'd missed? I closed it and
looked at the front cover, which was decorated with a line
drawing of a Zephyrcar humming along with its proud
owner looking deliriously happy. I glanced at the back
cover. All I saw there was the same old list of replacement
parts and a chart of service points. I'd read it at least a
dozen times before. It told what kind of air filter to get,
what kind of oil filter, stuff like that. It said what kind of
gasoline to put in the tank and what grade of oil to— Gasoline!

"Of course!" I yelled, giving myself a smack in the head
for being so dumb.

I grabbed the gas can we used for the lawn mower and
shook it. There was a sloshing inside. I undid the cap on the
Hovercraft tank and poured the gas in.

Once again, with rising hope, I braced my foot, grasped
the handle of the starting rope, and pulled.

Rrrr. Sput, sput.

I took a deep breath and pulled again.

Rrrrrrr. Sput, rrr, sput, sput.

"Come on, baby, kick in," I begged.

I braced both feet, locked my shoulders, and then—
pulled.

Rrrrrrr. Sput, rrrrr, sput, rrrrrrrr-RRRR!

The engine was roaring beautifully. It worked! It was
running as smooth as cream with a low, sweet sound like
tearing silk. It was beautiful! I knew just how Henry Ford
must have felt.

Then, nervously, I pulled the lever that engaged the pro-
peller drive shaft.

Crossing my fingers, I edged the lever over and forward.

And with a sudden whoosh, I felt a rush of wind come out of the bottom of my Hovercraft.

It worked! The engine drove the propellers and the propellers filled the plenum chamber and the wind rushed out. It would fly! I knew it!

Now, for the most incredible debut in the history of Carlyle. And for only fifty cents a ticket. I could hardly wait. Why, I'd sell hundreds!

6

As a matter of fact, I sold eleven.

I think that maybe a lot of people didn't believe me. It was probably too astounding for them to accept. I mean the idea of an ordinary seventh-grade semigenius assembling his own Zephyrcar and all. Pretty incredible when you think about it.

It's also possible some people didn't care, of course. Too apathetic. Some people wouldn't look up from watching re-runs of "Gilligan's Island" if Martians landed in their own backyard.

Whatever the reason, only eleven people bought tickets. That included the weird guy who lived on Brocklehurst Street, a guy everybody calls Fred even though his name is David. You'd think that if your name was David, you might say something if everybody called you Fred. But not him. He doesn't seem to care very much what he gets called. But he did have sense enough to buy a ticket, so maybe he's more normal than everybody thinks.

I ended up with an audience of fifteen. Pat and Kevin wouldn't buy a ticket. They insisted that I'd lied to them, telling them that it was a washing machine, and that they deserved to see it take off for free to make up for such a dirty trick. I tried to be reasonable and point out that they were the ones who said it was a washer, not me. But they wouldn't listen to reason. Personally, I think they were jealous. So finally we made a deal. I let them attend for free on the condition that they would help me carry the Zephyrcar from the garage out to the front yard. Which they did. Sort of.

Actually we found that we couldn't get it off the ground—it was too heavy.

"Why don't you just fly it down where you want it?" Pat suggested.

"Because that'd ruin the show," I explained. "People paid good money to see the Zephyrcar take off for the first time. At least," I added, giving both Pat and Kevin a sharp look, "some people paid good money. And it'd be a cheat if I fly it down there."

"Well, then bring them up here to the garage," Kevin said.

"Are you kidding?" I hooted. "It'd ruin the mood!"

"Oh, mood shmood," Pat said. "All I know is that there's no way the three of us can carry that thing."

"There has to be a way," I said.

"Too bad it doesn't have wheels," Kevin said. "We could just roll it down the driveway."

"That's it!" I shouted. "Wheels. We'll just put wheels on it."

"Sure, Albert," Pat said. "That'll only take about another week or two. What do we do with the people waiting there?" He nodded his head toward the front yard, where the ticket holders were already gathering. "Set up tents and breadlines for them?"

"Not permanent wheels," I explained. "Temporary ones. Just to get it down the driveway." I picked up an old automobile jack, a couple of two-by-fours and two old skateboards—all junk that had just been sitting in the garage.

"All we do is jack up one side of it," I said, "then slide one of the boards underneath it and rest each end of the board on a skateboard. Then we jack up the opposite side, slide the other board under, and rest that on the skateboards. And then we roll it down the driveway."

"Hmmm. Might work," Kevin said.

"It's worth a try," Pat added.

"Then let's do it," I exclaimed.

And we did.

As we rolled my beautiful new Zephyrcar down the driveway to its first flight, I had a tingling feeling in my stomach. Somehow things just seemed to be going my way.

Everything looked great. The new grass had started to come up really well, probably because of all the rain we'd been having, and the purple aluminum of the Zephyrcar looked good against the soft green background. I wasn't worried about damaging the grass when I took off, of course, because a Hovercraft doesn't exert much pressure at all on the ground when it's flying. It'd do less damage than a person's footsteps.

All eleven of my paying customers were there, plus Pat and Kevin. That made thirteen—which maybe should have told me something.

With everybody helping, we lifted the Zephyrcar off its wheels and set it down on the grass. Then, just about the time I was ready to start the ceremonies, Greta El Grosso and Bobby, the Bargain Basement Boyfriend, drove up in his Goodwill Industries Galaxie.

"Hey, it's Tom Swift and his flying cabbage picker," Greta said.

Naturally Bobby thought that was hilarious. I suppose

one or two others might have managed to crack a smile, too. I just ignored her.

"What's this," she said. "The big takeoff? Too bad you don't know your numbers to ten yet, or you could have a real countdown."

"Do you have tickets?" I asked frostily.

"Not for this fiasco," Greta sneered.

"This event is only for ticket holders and invited guests."

"I don't have to leave. I live here, Tom Swift. Or should I say, Tom Slow?" She looked around for approval, but nobody laughed at that one because it wasn't funny. Well, Bobby laughed, but he's nobody.

"Hey!" she screeched suddenly, her eyes bulging like boiled eggs. "Isn't that my skateboard over there?"

The way she was acting, you'd have thought I used her one and only pair of panty hose to make a tail for my kite. She hadn't been on that skateboard in years. I doubt that she even remembered she had it until she saw it there.

"Listen," she said, "if you're going to use my skateboard, without even asking my permission, then I certainly have the right to stand here on my very own front lawn and watch you blow yourself up."

"All right, all right," I muttered. Then I turned to the crowd. "Ladies and gentlemen," I said in a dignified manner, "please excuse my sister's behavior. My parents will be sending her back to the Home for the Ugly very soon."

That got a really big laugh, but it reminded me of something. My parents! I knew they'd want to see this. Unfortunately, Dad was off playing tennis. But my mother was home, working in the studio. So I told everybody I'd be back in a second and ran into her studio.

"I'm going to take off in my Zephyrcar now, Mom. You want to watch?"

She looked a little startled, like maybe she hadn't realized how far things had progressed. But she recovered quickly. "Yes, I do, Albert. I'd like to watch very much. Can you wait a sec, though? I'm trying to straighten up the studio. Mrs. Morgeld is coming over in a few minutes to look at my recent work and talk about sponsoring a one-woman show for me. Isn't that exciting?"

I went back outside and stalled around a little more. I tried to sell a few extra raffle tickets for a free ride. The tickets were only a dime each and I'd already sold twenty-seven, almost half of them to the guy named David called Fred. I planned on holding the raffle drawing right after the launch and demonstration flight.

But finally I couldn't stall any longer. I had to do something and it looked like my mother wasn't going to be coming out in time to watch. Oh well, I thought. She'll·have plenty of chances to see it later, on days when there isn't any Mrs. Morgeld to worry about.

"Ladies and gentlemen," I cried, "the big moment has come. This is a day, an hour, a minute that will be part of Carlyle's history for as long as people live here. As you know, I have been devoting all my time recently to building a revolutionary new kind of vehicle. One that travels on a velvety smooth cushion of air, floating along like the fabled magic carpet of the Arabian Nights . . ."

"Just fly it, Albert," Kevin said.

I gave him a dirty look, because I'd written and memorized a decent speech for the occasion. But now that he'd interrupted, I found I couldn't remember all of it.

". . . the Arabian Nights of old," I said. "And, uh, although this looks like a magical work of . . . er, of magic, it's really just the beginning of a new age of travel that will stretch from here all the way to . . . uh . . . all the way from here to . . . there. And beyond. So I welcome you to—"

"Fly it, Albert!" Pat shouted. "Or else give us our money back."

"All right, all right," I muttered. Man, the nerve of that Salerno, demanding his money back when he hadn't even paid any.

I braced myself, grasped the rope, and yanked.

Rrrrr-RRRR!

She started right up like a champ. The tank was full of gas and she was raring to go.

I have to admit that my stomach was fluttering a little as I climbed into the seat. Part of it was from joy—I was so happy that I'd really done it. And part of it was nerves. I settled myself, cinched the seat belt nice and tight, and grasped the control lever. Mentally I reviewed the instructions. They were simple. All I had to do was engage the propellers by shifting the transmission lever, and I'd lift off the ground about a foot, floating in mid-air. Then I'd use the joy stick to steer myself. A few quick loops up and down the block, and I'd land to uproarious applause.

Everybody was watching intently. They had formed a ring around me, standing about ten feet back from the Zephyrcar. Nobody said anything, not even Greta.

Just then a huge blue Mercedes pulled up and an old lady with silver hair got out. I glanced at her briefly, then put her out of my thoughts.

"All right, everybody," I yelled over the engine's purr, "get ready for the most amazing experience of your lives!"

Slowly I slipped the transmission lever over and forward. I heard a whoosh.

And then suddenly, before I knew what was happening to

me, I was spinning in circles, around and around, faster and faster. People's faces were whirling past so fast they looked distorted, like they were melting.

People screamed. Mud and grass flew everywhere.

Whipping past on one of my revolutions, I saw Greta open her mouth to holler just in time to get hit smack in the face with a baseball-sized dollop of mud. Another hunk of mud hit David called Fred on his left ear so it looked like he was wearing one brown ear muff. And another blob hit the old lady with the silver hair, splattering all over the front of her.

Out of all the confusion, rising above the din, I could hear a woman's voice yelling, "Turn it off! Turn it off!"

I was beginning to get so dizzy and sick to my stomach that I thought I'd faint, but finally I managed to grab hold of the lever somehow and slip it out of gear.

Immediately the Zephyrcar stopped spinning itself into the ground. The engine hiccuped once and died.

I looked around. Through swimming vision I could see that my audience was covered with mud and little blades of new grass.

My mother was trying to wipe off the old lady's dress and hair, saying, "Oh, Mrs. Morgeld, I'm so sorry. I'm so terribly sorry!"

I staggered out of the Zephyrcar and wobbled a few feet across what used to be our front yard. I didn't know what to do or say. I felt I should reassure them somehow.

Finally, I just said, "Well, how about that!" And then I asked in as cheerful a tone as I could muster, "Well, shall we see who won that raffle now?"

Everybody began to run. Except me.

I just threw up.

7

My father was shaking his tennis racket at me.

And yelling.

My mother was slumped in a chair, her face set in anger, her fingers knotted in her hair.

Greta was there, too.

"Do you know what the lawn cost us?" my father hollered. "And you've ruined it! And what's worse, you could have killed somebody out there!" He turned away from me and paced across the living room, then back again. I didn't know what to say to him.

"I wouldn't be surprised if Mrs. Morgeld had all my paintings burned now," my mother groaned. "The poor old woman nearly fainted. She thought she was being attacked by a runaway lawn mower."

I didn't know what to say to her, either.

"Well, it splattered mud and grass all over my face and hair," whined Greta.

I did have a good answer for that, but decided it'd be better to keep my mouth shut.

My father stopped in front of me, glaring. He was silent for a long time. He just stood there, chopping the neck of his tennis racket into the palm of his hand. I wondered what was going through his head. Was he reviewing the penalties for decapitating a twelve-year-old who destroys a newly seeded front lawn?

At last he said in a calmer voice, "What were all those people doing there?"

"Most of them bought tickets," I said.

"They bought tickets to get splattered with our new lawn?"

"Well, no. To see the first flight of my Zephyrcar. And they didn't all have tickets. Greta and Bobby came crashing in and wouldn't pay, and Pat and Kevin didn't pay, and that old lady, Mrs. Morgeld, didn't have a ticket. She just drove up by accident."

Dad gave his head a shake, as though to clear it, and then asked, "So what happened?"

I shrugged. I thought. I relived the whole experience—for about the nineteenth time.

"I don't know, Dad. I started the engine and it ran perfectly. It had plenty of gas and it sounded fine. Then I got on board and I fastened my seat belt, and then I engaged the lever to drive the propellers. The propellers should have spun around, creating lots of air pressure in the plenum chamber, and then it should have lifted off."

"I knew we never should have let him buy it," my mother said. "I told you it was a mistake."

"If you ask me, he's got air in his plenum chamber," Greta muttered.

My father looked at them vacantly and nodded faintly, but said nothing.

"Anyway, so that's what should have happened. But instead it started whirling around like a maniac merry-go-round and digging its way toward China. I almost got killed, Dad," I said plaintively, "and I don't know why it happened."

"He's too young to be fooling around with machinery like that," my mother said to my father.

"When I was his age I rebuilt a '48 Packard, so it's not that he couldn't have done it."

I became aware of a slight swing in moods. Nothing major, just a tiny something in the atmosphere. It seemed that since my mother was angry at both my father and me, that sort of made Dad and me allies. Maybe there was light at the end of this tunnel after all.

"Everything was working all right until you moved that lever? Is that right?"

I nodded.

Greta and Mom suddenly realized what was happening.

"Daddy!" Greta wailed. "Aren't you going to punish him? Golly!" she howled like a coyote, "if I did that you'd hang me up by my thumbs."

"Don't tell me that Albert's not going to be punished over this," my mother said firmly. "Because if you won't do it, I will! He nearly killed poor Mrs. Morgeld with mud and fright! Not to mention the other children who were there! And he's probably ruined any chance I might have had of getting Mrs. Morgeld to sponsor my exhibition!"

But Dad just said, "It was an accident. It wasn't entirely his fault. Albert, I think it'd be only fair if you paid to have the lawn reseeded. You can use your Uncle Albert's money to pay for it. And you'll have to call Mrs. Morgeld, tell her who you are, apologize, and offer to pay her cleaning bills. And refund all the ticket money you collected. Is all of that clear?"

I nodded. My heart had risen out of my shoes and felt buoyant again. I wasn't home free, but I hadn't suffered any serious damage to my posterior region, either.

56

"All right, then," he said. "Let's go out to the garage. There's something we have to do out there."

Boom! My heart fell right through my stomach and landed down around my ankles again. Here it comes, I thought. The old oak paddle.

Dad walked to the garage.

And the condemned boy trudged along behind him.

"Albert," Dad said, "I want you to bend over and—"

"Dad, wait a minute, please. You said yourself that it wasn't entirely my fault. Isn't that right?"

"Yeah. That's right. Now, bend over and—"

"No, no, wait. We need to talk about this. And you said that you rebuilt a car. But I'll bet you had some problems with that, didn't you?"

"Sure. Now, bend—"

"Well, gosh, Dad, I'd love to hear more about that. A Packard? How did you rebuild it? Where did you get the parts?"

"Albert, what is the matter with you? I'm starting to lose patience! I don't have all day, you know. Now, please bend over and look underneath your Zephyrcar for damage. Tell me how bad the propellers look, all right?"

"Huh?"

"Please, Albert?" Dad looked a little sheepish. "I'm sort of curious about what happened. I'd look under there myself, but I wrenched my back playing tennis this morning. So take a look, okay? Maybe together we can figure out what went wrong."

He didn't have to say any more. I got down and peered under the rubberized skirting at the propellers while he thumbed through the instruction manual. The propellers looked nicked, but they weren't broken as far as I could tell. I was probably lucky that the ground had been so soft and muddy—the mud may have been harder on the spectators, but it was definitely easier on the Zephyrcar. While I was looking at the underside, my father began reading the manual. When I looked up again he was as engrossed in the set of instructions as he would have been in a novel. Every so often he'd grunt or say "Hmmm, that's interesting." After several minutes he looked up and said, "Well? How's it look?"

"Muddy. But I can't see anything broken."

He nodded and thought for a moment, "Okay, good. Let's try to figure out what went wrong." And then, to himself, he said, "It looks like it ought to work."

We pulled the Zephyrcar apart and Dad began looking through the drivetrain. It was a complicated thing that was supposed to transmit power from the engine to the propellers, which would then spin around, creating lots of air pressure under the base of the Zephyrcar and causing the whole thing to lift off the ground. That was the theory, at least.

In about twenty minutes Dad found something.

"Look, here," he said. "This transpositional gear is in backward. So when you started the engine and engaged the propellers, they were spinning in the wrong direction, creating a suction instead of a lift. You were pulling yourself down instead of pushing yourself up."

It took us about three hours to take the gear out and put it back in right, but we finally did it.

"Considering how complicated this thing is," Dad said, "you did a great job of assembling it. It's too bad about the accident, but it's a rare bird that flies the first time out.

Believe me, son—we've had plenty of initial disasters at Aerotech that eventually flew like eagles."

That made me feel a little better about having made a mistake. Maybe I wasn't such an idiot after all.

"We're not going to have time to test it today," Dad said, motioning toward the sky. "It's getting dark. But tomorrow we'll see what happens. All right?"

Early the next morning after I delivered my papers, Dad and I rented a U-Haul trailer and a power jack. We used the jack to lift the Zephyrcar into the trailer. My mother was pretty annoyed and muttered something about "crazy engineers and engineers' kids" that I didn't quite catch. I don't think my father heard it, either, because he seemed pretty jolly. After a quick breakfast we drove out to an open field near Lunken Airport, about five miles from home. We unloaded the Zephyrcar on a dirt road that was heavily rutted and a little smushy from all the rain.

I felt even more nervous than I had the previous day. Then I'd been too dumb to realize that something could go wrong. Now I felt pretty certain that nothing would go right. What if the thing blew up this time?

My father adjusted the linkage again and checked the whole thing over one more time. He seemed to read my thoughts.

"Don't worry," he said. "You made a little mistake with that gear, but everything's going to work great now."

I just shrugged and said, "Guess we'll never know unless we give it a try."

"There you go," he said, giving me an encouraging pat on the back. "Well, fire when ready, Gridley."

I braced myself and pulled the rope. The engine fired

right up. It still had plenty of gasoline in it—tearing up the lawn hadn't used very much.

I got into the seat and fastened my seat belt. Then I grasped the lever. My stomach felt queasy.

I looked at my father. He smiled and gave me a thumbs-up sign for good luck.

Slowly, I eased the lever over and forward. I felt a slight *thump* down below as the propellers kicked in.

For a moment nothing happened.

And then, suddenly, the whole thing lifted gently off the ground.

It worked! My Hovercraft was hovering! My Zephyrcar was zephing!

It's hard to remember much about my first few minutes of flight. I was so excited that my brain apparently ceased to function normally, completely unplugging the memory portion. I remember being astonished at how smoothly the Zephyrcar moved. Except for the feeling of air brushing past my face and a vague buzzing sensation in my rear from the engine's vibration, I had no sense of motion at all.

At first I oversteered the Zephyrcar, yanking the control lever hard to make it turn. But eventually I found that it responded much better to gentle, gradual motions. And at first I had a tendency to lean in the direction I wanted to go, but I found that leaning actually slowed the Zephyrcar down because it raised one edge of the plenum chamber too high and we lost compression. What I learned was that by staying calm and moving the controls smoothly, I got the best performance.

I flew it around for a couple of hours that morning, growing more and more comfortable with it, until a light rain began to fall and we decided to go home.

We tried lots of interesting things, though, before we

quit. After it took off the first time and I had flown it around for awhile, Dad wanted to try it. He didn't say that he did. But he was bouncing up and down and looking more excited than a kid on Christmas morning, so I stopped it and invited him to take a ride.

But when he got on, it wouldn't go. The engine was still running all right, but it wouldn't lift off.

"Maybe it doesn't like you," I suggested.

"More likely it doesn't like my weight." My father is six feet tall and weighs about a hundred and eighty. About seventy pounds more than me.

He looked awfully disappointed, and I felt sorry for him. "Maybe you can lose some weight, Dad," I said.

"I've got a feeling the only way I could lose enough would be amputation," he said, "and I'm not that eager to ride a Hovercraft."

Another thing we found was that the Zephyrcar had a tendency to kick up a small cloud of dirt as it went along. A few specks got in my eyes and nose, and my clothes were pretty well coated. My father suggested that for safety I should wear some kind of goggles or helmet, and I agreed. I'd probably be a lot more comfortable, too.

One more thing we discovered was that the Zephyrcar was hard to turn. There was a steering lever that altered the pitch of the propellers, thus changing the pressure of the air cushion and moving the Zephyrcar in whatever direction I wanted to go. But it only worked when I leaned heavily in that direction, tilting the opposite edge of the plenum chamber slightly off the ground. At best, steering was imprecise.

But none of that mattered. The important thing was that it worked. And I planned to use it the very next morning to deliver my papers.

I could hardly wait to get to Sycamore Hill Road.

That afternoon I tried to repair the previous day's damage.

The most embarrassing thing I had to do was call Mrs. Morgeld, explain who I was, and apologize. She was pretty decent about it—aloof but decent—and graciously estimated the amount of the bill for having her dress drycleaned. I also offered to come over to her house and wash her Mercedes for her, but she nixed that idea right away.

I didn't even try to explain to the nursery what had happened to the lawn. I just told them there had been an accident and part of it had to be reseeded. They were agreeable and told me what it would cost.

When it was all finally done—when I'd apologized to everybody, paid all the bills, returned all the money, and generally tried to redeem myself—I began to see that owning a Zephyrcar just might be more complicated and expensive than I had anticipated.

My ledger now looked like this:

Income and Expenses		
3/7 Check from good old Uncle Albert		$1000.00
4/6 One Zephyrcar!!!		$563.79
Balance Left	$436.21	
4/28 Tickets for Launching: 11 at $.50 =	$5.50	
Raffle tickets for ride: 27 at $.10 =	$2.70	
New Balance	$444.41	
4/30 Refund ticket money		$8.20
Dry cleaning (Mrs. Morgeld's dress)		$12.00
Reseeding the lawn		$97.63
Balance Left	$326.58	

8

I got up at the usual time, half-past five, and rolled out of bed. The floor was cold and the sky was still black outside, but I was very excited. I'd have been eager to deliver the papers even if there'd been two feet of snow on the ground.

The previous night I'd put together a Zephyrcar uniform to protect me from the mud and dust and twigs. To cover my head and face I took an old football helmet from the bottom of the toy box down in the basement, spray-painted it purple to match the color of the Zephyrcar, and then rigged up a piece of red, translucent plastic around the front of the helmet. I put on a blue ski jacket, a pair of blue sweatpants that I'd used the previous summer at Y Camp, and a pair of my father's old work gloves that were enormous. Finally, over my shoulders I draped a canvas bag suspended from two ropes. I adjusted the ropes so that the bag hung about stomach high. That was for the papers.

I also made one change on the Zephyrcar, at my father's urging. It was a good idea. He'd been worried that drivers might not see me in the early hours and that I might get hit. So he'd asked me to put some lights on the Zephyrcar. Unfortunately, the only lights I'd been able to find were the Christmas tree lights out in the garage. I wired them into the Zephyrcar's system and found (to my dismay) when I turned them on that they blinked.

As I walked through the dark kitchen with my helmet tucked under my elbow, I looked outside. It was raining steadily. I groaned a little, but even a typhoon wouldn't have been enough to dampen my spirits this morning.

After grabbing a quick snack of four powdered sugar donuts and some orange juice, I got a big umbrella out of the closet. I didn't see any reason why I couldn't hold the umbrella and steer the Hovercraft with one hand, and toss newspapers with the other. That was something I never could have done on my bike, of course, but it didn't seem like it would be too hard with the old Zephyrcar.

The motor started right up; I put it in gear and sailed out of the garage on a cushion of air. I turned up Rose Avenue and whirred along to Sixth Street, where I always picked up my papers.

As I drew closer, through the dim light of the street lamps and the blur of the light rain, I could see Morris's car alongside the curb. Its headlights were still on and I could hear its low rumble as it sat there idling.

But when I pulled up, there were no papers and no Morris, either. I sat there, hovering in the Zephyrcar, looking around.

"Morris?" I called softly. "Morris, are you here?"

I heard another sound, sort of a strangled *"Aaw-ough . . ."*

I shut off the Zephyrcar, climbed down, pulled off my helmet, and walked around to the rear of Morris's car. He was kneeling there, holding on to the bumper with both hands.

"Is that you, Albert?" he asked. The way he said it, you'd

have thought he was seeing the ghost of Christmas past or something.

"Yeah, it's me, Morris. Who else is going to be out here in the rain at five-forty-five in the morning? You got some papers for me?"

He nodded quickly and stood up. Then he saw the Zephyrcar sitting beside the curb in front of his car.

"That your vehicle, babe?" he asked.

I couldn't help smiling proudly. "Yeah, it's mine. I even made it. Well, really, I just put it together, but I did it myself. I'm going to fly it around to deliver my papers from now on. It floats on air."

"That right?" Morris said thoughtfully. He stared at it through narrowed eyes for several minutes. Then he asked, "Your folks know about this?"

"Oh sure, they know all about it. In fact, my dad helped me get it fixed up so it works just fine."

"That so?" Morris shook his head slowly and muttered, "No figuring out some folks at all."

He lifted my bundle of papers and plastic wrappers out of his trunk, dropping them on the sidewalk for me.

He started to get into his car, then paused and said, "New bike wouldn't be as good, huh?"

"No comparison, Morris."

"Yeah. Course you couldn't scare nobody out of his wits with a new bike, could you?" Then he got in the car and drove off.

As I folded and stuffed the papers I puzzled over his behavior. I was a little disappointed that he hadn't seemed more interested in my Zephyrcar, too, but maybe he was preoccupied.

I loaded the wrapped papers into my carrying bag, pulled the rope to start the engine, and climbed into the

Zephyrcar. Holding the umbrella and the steering lever in my left hand, I prepared to throw papers with my right.

I headed up Sixth, umbrella over my head, Christmas lights blinking. As I neared my first house I maneuvered up onto the sidewalk and got ready to throw a paper.

But right away I found I had a problem. I couldn't drive down the sidewalk and hold the umbrella without bumping into things. First I bumped into a tree. It was just a glancing jolt along the side of the Zephyrcar, but it spun me a quarter of the way around just at the moment I threw the paper. Instead of sailing toward the Oxenhams' front porch, it sailed up the sidewalk to land with a soft plop in a puddle.

Things quickly got out of hand. I collided with mailboxes, a low white picket fence, and accidentally flew over Mrs. Ziegler's flower bed, chopping all her tulips to red and yellow confetti.

I tried to maneuver out into the street, where I'd have more room to move around, but then I found I couldn't get the papers up to the porches. Maybe if I just throw harder, I thought, I can get them up there. But I ended up putting the MacPhersons' paper in their hedge and the Cantanellis' on their roof. Besides which my shoulder was starting to ache.

Then I got a good idea. Why not go up the street, turn into each driveway, throw the paper, then back out of the driveway and go on to the next house?

I tried it with the next couple of houses and it worked really well. The only problem was at the Nibleys' and I really don't think it was entirely my fault. After all, they were the ones who left their garbage cans out, not me. All I did was fly into them with my Zephyrcar.

But that was all I had to do, I guess, because I knocked

three of them over. The clatter they made sounded like an explosion. And what was worse, they began rolling downhill. It wasn't much of a slope, not like Sycamore Hill Road, but it was enough to keep those cans going.

Well, I just couldn't let the Nibleys' garbage cans roll away, especially when they were booming like drums. So I leaped off the Zephyrcar and began to chase them. Unfortunately, I forgot to turn off the Zephyrcar—I was too used to riding a bicycle, I suppose, which doesn't keep driving all over town when you get off it. But a Zephyrcar will keep driving, or flying. It went right up the driveway again, through a rose hedge—the sound of those branches snapping off was horrible—and up against a tall tree, where it began to circle around and around the trunk, its multicolored Christmas lights winking on and off.

Suddenly there was an enormous crash from down the road. I looked in time to see a car roar away from the intersection where it had unexpectedly been greeted by three rolling garbage cans. The car kept on going. But those cans, I could tell, would never roll again.

After school I visited Mrs. Ziegler and the Nibleys. I just told them I'd had an accident and offered to pay for the damages. Happily they didn't quiz me about how the accident had happened.

That night I made some new entries in my ledger:

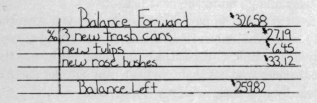

	Balance Forward	$326.58
⁹⁄₆₃	3 new trash cans	$27.19
	new tulips	$6.45
	new rose bushes	$33.12
	Balance Left	$259.82

68

Well, you have to figure that the first flight of any aircraft will have a few problems. I've heard my dad say that lots of times. I hoped that things would improve, that they'd get better the next day and the next and the next, until flying my Zephyrcar to deliver the papers became the easiest, most natural thing in the world.

It wasn't raining the next morning, so I didn't have to put the papers in wrappers or carry an umbrella. I just loaded up my canvas bag and started out.

I felt that I had finally mastered the art of ducking in and out of driveways and flipping the papers while flying. I could hardly wait for Sycamore Hill Road. The previous day I'd been too upset about the rose bushes and trash cans to appreciate the ride up the hill. This morning I intended to savor it.

I didn't have long to wait. Soon it loomed before me, the Mount Everest of Carlyle, Ohio. But I felt like Sir Edmund Hillary, the first westerner to conquer Everest. So it was an even match this morning.

We began the long climb. I felt fine all the way up. I flipped papers to the Jacobsons' and the Emersons' and the Kaplans' and I wasn't even breathing hard. The old Zephyrcar was zipping along, the Christmas lights were blinking merrily, the papers were flying accurately. When I got to old lady Liffy's house, I was having a little trouble seeing clearly because of the moisture inside my red visor. I pulled into her driveway, flipped her paper, heard it clunk on her porch, then backed out of her driveway and started up the rest of the hill. Faintly, a strange gurgling noise seemed to come from the house. What the heck was that?

I stopped and hovered in the middle of the street. I looked toward her house again and thought I saw a shape in her upstairs window for a second. But that's all I saw or heard.

When I finished my deliveries on the hill and reached the top, I paused as I usually did. But this time I paused to gloat, not to keep my heart from exploding from overwork. At last, I had conquered that crummy hill.

Carefully putting the lever into a neutral position—a lesson I had learned yesterday—I climbed out of the Hovercraft. I stood at the brow of the hill, my fists on my hips and my feet planted firmly, and I looked down at the river. It was gray and swollen and moving rapidly. As I stared down at it from the peak of Sycamore Hill Road, I decided I didn't feel like Hillary after all. I felt like Cortés—the Spanish conqueror of Mexico.

Except that Cortés didn't hear police sirens in the background and I did. What could Baloney Jack be up to? It was rare to hear police sirens ever in Carlyle, but especially at six-thirty in the morning.

Down in the valley I could see the flashing blue lights of the cruiser tearing through the housing district. The siren's scream rose and fell. I thought about the shape I had glimpsed at Miss Liffy's window and the noise I had heard.

The morning was creeping up over the Kentucky hills, on the eastern side of the river, and I knew I had to finish my route as quickly as possible. But I couldn't help being curious. I decided to take a quick peek at what was going on, and then hurry and finish my route.

When I got to Ninth, I left the Zephyrcar in neutral again and cut through a couple of backyards.

The police cruiser was parked in front of Miss Liffy's place. A policeman—it was Baloney Jack, all right—was talking to Miss Liffy on her porch, taking notes as she talked.

I crouched behind some bushes to listen. It was hard to hear with the helmet, but I caught most of their conversation.

"So it wasn't a robber, Miss Liffy?" he asked.

"No, it wasn't a robber. Did I say it was a robber?" she snapped.

"Yes, ma'am, on the phone you did."

"Well, of course I did on the phone, you fool," she said, "because if I told you what I really saw you wouldn't have come. But it wasn't any robber!"

The policeman sighed. "Then what was it, Miss Liffy?"

"I saw a UFO!" she announced.

"A what!?" he exclaimed, obviously displeased. I looked up in the sky, which was already pale from the coming dawn. There was nothing there right now.

Suddenly I remembered the noise. Had that been the UFO? Or Miss Liffy crying out in fright? Was that when she'd seen it? Maybe I could have seen it, too! I began to feel kind of creepy and edgy. I looked around nervously. The bushes rustled slightly, the dark pockets of night seemed to shift uneasily.

"What did it look like, Miss Liffy?" asked Baloney Jack. He stifled a big yawn.

"You wouldn't be yawning if you'd seen it, John Bannigore," Miss Liffy snarled. "Now you write this down and get it right so when it jumps out of the sky and lands on your police car you'll recognize it."

"Yes, ma'am," he said.

"It was about the size of a full-grown female gorilla," she said. "Only it had enormous, ferocious-looking hands, and an enormous round head with a reddish, blank face. Ugh—it was horrible!"

I could hear the shudder in her voice and it made me

shudder, too. Except that something in that description sounded awfully familiar.

"What kind of vehicle was this alien using? Or was it just walking down the street?" asked the policeman.

"Of course it wasn't walking, you overgrown goose! It was flying on a flying saucer. A purple flying saucer about the size of a golf cart without wheels."

"It was in a flying golf cart? Was it the kind with the fringed canopy or not?"

She started to tell him off again for being so dense, but I didn't need to hear any more. I knew what she'd seen. She'd seen me!

I was the alien in my own hometown!

I leaped to my feet and tried to tiptoe away, but I tripped on a root and cried out. Both Miss Liffy and Baloney Jack ran to the end of her porch in time to see me scramble to my feet and run away.

"Aargh!" Miss Liffy screamed. "It's the being! Look!"

"Well, I'll be darned!" Baloney Jack exclaimed.

I heard his shout and then I heard his running feet. But I didn't look back. I was too scared.

Now if I'd had any sense, I would have stopped and said, "Hi everybody. I'm Albert Halperin and I'm delivering papers in my Zephyrcar suit." But with old lady Liffy so upset that she was nearly hysterical, and with Baloney Jack obviously irritated at being pulled out before the sun was even up and then being made a fool of, I figured I was in trouble. So I ran.

I jumped back into my Zephyrcar and was glad I'd left the engine running. I jammed it into gear, lifted off, and headed back up the alley. I just wanted to get away from there.

As I zoomed up the alley I heard a peal of sirens and a

screech of tires. Above the rooftops I saw the glow of flashing blue lights. I crossed Ninth Street and continued up the alley just as the cruiser came roaring up Ninth. I thought for a moment he hadn't seen me, but then I heard his brakes scream.

Officer Bannigore must have made a U-turn on Ninth Street, because in less than thirty seconds he was roaring up the alley, lights flashing, no more than a hundred yards behind me.

I looked to the left, but saw the brick fence behind the Watsons' house. To the right was an open backyard. I leaned that way and yanked on the steering lever. I floated across the grass, and then across something else that I couldn't make out in the dim light. It was rectangular and flat and grayish. And then I could tell I was over grass again.

The flashing lights were right behind me and then the police car turned. Its glaring headlights caught me. The sirens were wailing and lights were snapping on all over the neighborhood. The cruiser was only fifty or sixty feet behind me and closing fast.

"You know, Albert," I said to myself, "this is very foolish. You should just stop and explain things in a reasonable manner to Officer Bannigore. You can have a quiet chuckle over it together and then he can run you through the burger grinder at Mickelmeier's Meats."

So I stopped the Zephyrcar and climbed down to face him.

But just as I did, there was a tremendous splash and I whirled around barely in time to see Carlyle's only police cruiser sinking into that gray rectangle—a swimming pool. It was very interesting to watch the blue lights flash under water. Rather artistic looking, actually.

Officer Bannigore swam out the window on the driver's side and did the back stroke to the edge of the pool. He pulled himself out and kneeled on the grass, shivering.

Then he saw me standing there.

"Ah!" he yelped. "Don't hurt me! Please!" His hands were clasped together. "I'm a friend. Friend! Peace!"

A small crowd of people in robes and pajamas had gathered at various corners of the yard, peering around things, curious about what was going on but none too eager to get any closer.

I raised my arms and held out both hands toward him.

"Peace to you, too, earthling—or whatever you are."

And then I took off for home.

9

The next day there was a special edition of the *Hill-topper*. That was news in itself, because the *Hilltopper* is just a bi-weekly throwaway paper, the kind that gets delivered in a plastic bag hung over your doorknob, along with grocery store ads and flyers announcing new nursery schools. It's not a real newspaper—a daily—like the one I deliver.

So a special edition was rather sensational. And I had a hunch that I knew what had caused it. After all, the *Courier* is edited and printed by Edward Bannigore at his Quickee Print shop down at the Western Islands Mall. Patrolman John B. just happens to be his son.

I unfolded the paper with curiosity and anticipation. And I wasn't disappointed. Across the top of the front page a banner headline screamed:

ALIEN BEING ATTACKS CARLYLE COP! ! !

That seemed a bit exaggerated to me. But then they were the ones who were writing the paper, not me. The article continued in the same hysterical tone as the headline:

In what may be the most remarkable incident in the history of Carlyle, an alien being attacked a local police officer during the pre-dawn hours.

> The attack was witnessed by several local residents, and
> the being was observed twice by Miss Arville Liffy, a longtime
> Carlyle resident, who lives at 983 Sycamore Hill Road.

And so it went, talking about the sighting, describing what
Miss Liffy had seen, how she had called the police, everything. It even included a description of the dredging opera-
tion used to pull the car out of the pool. There were some
photographs of Deputy Bannigore and old Miss Liffy and
the pool. And one other thing: There was an artist's concep-
tion of the alien being and of the UFO. Neither one of the
pictures was too great, since the *Hilltopper*'s staff artist
was thirteen-year-old Holly Bannigore, John's sister. The
alien being looked like a gingerbread man with a toothache.
Even a psychic wouldn't be able to tell it was really me. But
the flying saucer was another story. Even though she apparently drew the picture with blunt crayons, the flying
saucer looked . . . well, it looked like a Zephyrcar!

For several days I delivered my papers on my old bike
again. And tried to figure out what to do.

The whole town was talking about the UFO, but for-
tunately nobody seemed to notice the resemblance between
the flying saucer and my Zephyrcar. At least, I don't think
anybody noticed. The day after the *Hilltopper*'s special edition, my father looked at me with a twisty smile on his face
and said, "Be careful delivering your papers, son. Don't let
any UFO's get you."

Most people were of the opinion that Officer Bannigore
was probably playing the game with a few bolts loose. The
Cincinnati papers picked up the story right away, of
course, and began asking what Carlyle was putting in its
water supply, and whether the town was trying to compete
with King's Island as a tourist attraction, things like that.

After a week, though, people lost interest and went back to talking about the price of gas and the Reds' chances of winning the pennant. I figured it might be safe to take the Zephyrcar out again.

I left a little earlier than usual to avoid as much traffic as possible. Especially Officer Bannigore. He was back on the beat, driving the Mickelmeier's Meats delivery truck while the patrol car was drying out. But I figured that with any luck at all I could avoid him. The meat truck was a blue van with a six-foot sausage on the roof, so it was easy to spot. And I took the Christmas lights off the Zephyrcar and decided to forget the uniform, too, figuring that those changes would help make me less conspicuous.

Everything went fine for the first half of the route. I went past Miss Liffy's place as quietly as possible, of course. The windows stayed dark. No muffled cries emerged from the upper story windows, no sirens began wailing in the distance.

At the top of Sycamore Hill Road I turned down Ridgeway. The trash cans were out all along Ridgeway, because it was the morning when the Springer Sanitation Service made collections. In fact, I could see their big, old truck lumbering up the road about a block or two ahead of me.

It stopped at another house, wheezing from leaky air brakes, and the driver jumped out. He threw the bags of trash into the maw of the truck, emptied a can, then punched some controls on the side of the truck that made the big metal mouth slowly close, crunching the garbage back inside. There was the sound of hydraulics and then the thing opened up again, empty.

Meanwhile, I was floating down Ridgeway, flipping papers onto driveways and porches. The empty trash cans were just the teensiest bit of trouble to steer around. Otherwise, the morning was blissful.

Just as I was reflecting that there wasn't even any rain for once, I saw trouble pull off of McCracken Drive and onto Ridgeway in the form of a van with a giant sausage on its roof. It was heading straight toward me, and although it was still pretty dark, I figured Baloney Jack was bound to see me.

My one hope was to get up close behind the garbage truck and hide.

Jamming the stick forward, I sent the Zephyrcar zipping forward just as fast as it would go. The garbage truck had stopped at the next house, about thirty yards ahead of me. Baloney Jack was still a block and a half away. But he was really moving and he had his high beams on. It was going to be close.

The driver jumped out of the garbage truck again, swung around the side, and began throwing in bags of garbage. Just as he tossed in the last one and moved to the control panel, he happened to catch sight of me zooming down on him. His hand was poised, trembling, halfway to the controls. I waved one hand in a friendly gesture to let him know he was safe, that I wasn't going to crash into his truck or anything. But at the same instant Officer Bannigore roared up in the meat truck. He jammed on the brakes, leaped out in his complete policeman suit, pulled his gun, pointed it at me from around the rear of the truck, and shouted:

"Don't make a move, alien! I've got you covered!"

That did it. The astonished garbage man lurched against the side of his truck for support. But when he fell against the truck he must have hit the wrong button, because suddenly there was an enormous grinding of gears and then all three of us stood, wide-eyed and horrified, while the garbage truck raised itself skyward and dumped a cascade of banana peels, eggshells, coffee grounds, newspapers, scraps, trash, and junk all over Mickelmeier's meat truck, my Zephyrcar, the middle of Ridgeway Street, and the three of us.

"Give me the charges again," my father said to Officer Bannigore.

Baloney Jack, who had cleaned most of the garbage from his uniform some time earlier, ticked them off on his fingers as he spoke. "Impersonating an alien being. Operating an unidentified flying object without a license. Disturbing the peace. Damaging police property."

Dad nodded, looking at the mayor, who sat behind his desk. We had been called to a special session of Mayor's Court to answer the charges Officer Bannigore was filing.

"Maybe we could talk about each of those," Dad said, "one by one. All right?"

The mayor nodded. "That all right with you, Officer?"

Officer Bannigore looked annoyed, but he remembered he was a public servant and that the mayor was his boss, so he said, "Yes, sir."

"In the first place," Dad began, "no matter how odd Albert may act at times, he has never intentionally impersonated an alien being. And besides, what ordinance makes it illegal to impersonate an alien? Second, he wasn't operating a UFO without a license—not that UFO's are normally licensed in this state, anyway. He was operating a Hovercraft. Is there an ordinance on the books that says he has to have a license for it?"

The mayor looked at Officer Bannigore. "Well?" he asked somewhat curtly.

"Yes, sir, any wheeled vehicle, even a moped has to . . ."

"But what about unwheeled vehicles?" my father asked. "And it seems quite clear that the peace wasn't disturbed until you came roaring up and scared that poor garbage man half out of his skin. And as for damaging police property—who owns that hot dog wagon? The police? No, it belongs to Carl Mickelmeier. And it wasn't damaged, anyway, just dirtied. I think Albert would be happy to pay to have the truck washed. Wouldn't you, Albert?"

Dad nudged me.

"Yes, sir," I said quickly. "I'd be glad to pay for it, or even wash it myself."

The mayor sat quietly, his chin resting on his hand. Officer Bannigore's brows were knit together and his forehead was corrugated with wrinkles from the effort of thinking.

Finally he said, "Well, what about the damage to the police cruiser? You can't deny that it was damaged."

The mayor sat up and cleared his throat. "Officer Bannigore, do you really want the matter of the police cruiser investigated further?"

Baloney Jack thought about it awhile, and finally decided that perhaps his own behavior during that episode was best left unexamined. So he said, in a muffled voice, "No, sir, probably not."

"After all," the mayor said firmly, "it wasn't Albert who drove into that pool. Apparently he flew over it. It was you who decided to pursue him through a private citizen's backyard and ended up drowning the town's only patrol car."

The mayor's voice had risen slightly and his face reddened. Officer Bannigore looked sheepish, and I had the feeling he and the mayor had probably been through this before.

The mayor turned to Dad and me. "I have no choice but to dismiss these charges," he said, "mainly because none of them apply." Then he looked very intently at me. "But don't think I'm at all pleased about this uproar."

"Yes, sir," I said.

"All right, then. That's all," he said.

"Thanks," my father said, and I echoed him.

But Officer Bannigore shook his head. "I'll be looking into this," he said. Then he looked at me. "And I won't let it drop," he added menacingly.

10

On Thursday I picked up the regular edition of the *Hilltopper* and flipped through the pages, skipping over the minutes of various grade school PTA's and announcements of engagements, marriages, and babies. I wasn't interested in any of that.

I was interested in a short paragraph under the heading "Council Notes." The paragraph said:

> City Council also took up a proposed ordinance which would ban the operation of any air-cushioned vehicle of any size, shape, manufacture, or purpose within the city of Carlyle. Final action was delayed until next month's meeting.

Sighing, I crumpled the paper in my hand. I could see Officer Bannigore behind this proposed ordinance. The fact that final action was delayed was probably a technicality.

There were some other items in the Council Notes, too: a request from the owners of the Western Islands Shopping Mall for the city to reinforce the flood wall; a resolution from the Carlyle Cat Club to name June Adopt-a-Cat-Month in Carlyle; a reading by eighth-grader LaRue Lipp of her prize-winning essay, "Litter Less for a Clean Tomorrow."

Go get 'em, LaRue, I murmured to myself.

And then I had to chuckle because there wasn't a single mention in the entire *Hilltopper* of the biggest news story of the week—namely, the fact that Patrolman Bannigore had single-handedly captured the notorious Carlyle alien while driving the Mickelmeier's Meats delivery truck and in the process had managed to decorate the aforementioned truck, plus the alien's craft and the streets of Carlyle, with a full load of fresh garbage. And you'd have thought that the fact that they had to bring out the city's snow plow to scrape the garbage up would have been worth a snapshot or two, wouldn't you?

But there was nothing. There was, however, an interesting editorial. Normally the *Hilltopper* takes hard-hitting stands on such controversial topics as wearing seat belts and supporting the Girl Scouts. But this was different:

HOVERCRAFT HORROR

Carlyle citizens have recently been subjected to a rampage of attacks which have left many of our residents terrified to leave their homes.

These attacks have come not from organized bands of hoodlums, but rather from a lone marauder who strikes in the pre-dawn hours and who so far has taken advantage of loopholes in local law to roar around our quiet streets unchecked.

Obviously, the quicker Carlyle is rid of this Hovercraft horror, the safer and happier all of its residents will be. We commend our police department's vigilance in pursuing this fiend.

I personally thought it was a lousy editorial, but I admit I may have been somewhat prejudiced. After all, I'd never been singled out as a public menace before.

"Hovercraft horror," I muttered disgustedly. "Horse puckey!"

Outside, the rain was pouring down again. I couldn't help thinking that my Zephyrcar's future in Carlyle looked even bleaker than the weather.

During the next week or so that editorial's statement about our "police department's vigilance" proved to be a bit of an understatement. It would have been more accurate if it had mentioned Officer Bannigore's instinct for revenge: On Friday I was picked up and brought home to my parents, who were still groggy with sleep since it was six-twenty in the morning, and charged with driving without a license. One look at my father's face and Baloney Jack decided not to press charges.

On Saturday I was arrested and taken to the police department. Officer Bannigore was about to fingerprint me when I said, "Hey, don't I get one phone call first?"

I called my father and told him I'd been collared again.

"What's the charge this time?" he asked.

"I don't know. He didn't tell me yet."

"Well, ask him. You've got a right to know."

I covered the mouthpiece with my hand and turned to Officer Bannigore, who was getting the fingerprint kit out of the desk. "My dad wants to know what the charges are."

"Operating a scooter without a license," he said as he began to ink the pad.

"He says operating a scooter without a license," I told my father.

"Let me talk to him," he said wearily.

I held out the receiver. "Here," I said. "He wants to talk to you."

Officer Bannigore took the phone and looked at it as though he expected to see a tarantula on it. "Hello?" he said.

Five minutes later he hung up and said to me, "Go peddle your papers, kid."

On Sunday and Monday I didn't get arrested because Baloney Jack had those days off.

On Tuesday I didn't get arrested because I flew up and down the alleys and threw the papers onto people's back porches and patios.

On Wednesday I was arrested for flying without a proper license. He chickened out before we got back to my house. But thanks to all the rigmarole I was late to school and had to go into the principal's office with a note: "Please excuse Albert's tardiness, he was arrested again this morning."

That afternoon, after I came home from school, the doorbell rang. My mother and I nearly collided in the hall as we both went to answer it.

"It's probably Mrs. Morgeld to see me," she was saying as she opened the door.

Mrs. Morgeld was standing there on our doorstep, all right, and standing right next to her, elbowing her for room, was Officer Bannigore.

"Hello, Mrs. Morgeld," my mother said. "Hello, Mr. Bannigore. Are you here to arrest Albert again?"

Mrs. Morgeld had started to smile and say hello, but her face suddenly froze.

"Yes, ma'am," said Officer Bannigore.

"What is it this time?" my mother asked.

Baloney Jack opened a small black book. "According to section one-hundred-and-twenty-three point two nine of the Municipal Code of the City of Carlyle, Ohio, it is against the law to park a house trailer on a private driveway. Now, I believe that purple vehicle at the end of your driveway belongs to your son, one Albert Halperin, male Caucasian, age twe—"

"Mister Bannigore," my mother muttered between clenched teeth, "do you realize that this is the fourth time in a week that you have attempted to arrest my son?" Her voice began to rise toward hysteria. "And not once have you been able to make it stick! And you never will, copper! So get out of here before I do something violent."

"Yes, ma'am," he said hastily. He scrambled off the porch, then turned around and sprinted to his patrol car.

During this confrontation, Mrs. Morgeld's head had been snapping back and forth from my mother to Baloney Jack, a look of utter disbelief on her face.

My mother turned to her now and smiled sweetly. "Now, Mrs. Morgeld, won't you come in? We have so much to talk about."

And as Mrs. Morgeld entered, Mom turned to me and whispered hoarsely, "And I'll take care of you later, buster!"

I was shocked. I'd never heard her call me or anybody else "buster" before. But then I'd never heard her say "copper," either. It was mighty strong language for my mother.

". . . so then I had to explain to Mrs. Morgeld why he had been arrested four times in one week," my mother was telling my father at dinner that night, "and explaining it was almost worse than not saying anything more about it. She just looked at me like I was a talking ostrich and said, 'You artists lead such exciting lives.' "

"That's one word for it," my father said. "What kind of vegetables are these?"

"Samoan style," Mom said. "They're new."

"Hmm. They're pretty good," he said. "Can I have Samoa?"

Mom glared at him. "I'm not in the mood for silly puns

this evening. I mean, it's a wonder Mrs. Morgeld didn't decide to withdraw her support from my show."

"Well, I think it's getting ridiculous," Greta growled. "Thanks to him"—she jerked her head at me—"I'm the laughingstock of the whole school."

"Oh, don't thank me," I said. "It's nothing you couldn't have done all by yourself."

"She's right," my mother said to my father. "It's getting ridiculous. I'm about ready to consider sending him to military school!"

"In Australia, I hope," said Greta.

Dad sighed. "Well, Mrs. Morgeld is still going to sponsor your one-woman show, isn't she?"

Mom nodded. "It's all arranged for Saturday. But thanks to all this rain, a pipe's burst at the Back Street Gallery downtown. They've had to reschedule my show at the Florian—the gallery at the Western Islands Mall. Another shopping center exhibition!"

I could tell she was pleased, though. Even though it was in a shopping center, her exhibition would have a lot of prestige because it was being held inside a gallery, and not along the mall among plastic ferns and water fountains.

Dinner went quietly for a few minutes and then my sister suddenly piped up and said, "Hey! What about Albert and his machine? Are we sending him to Australia or not?"

Dad looked at her sharply and said, "We aren't doing anything of the kind. Your mother and I will decide what to do, but I'll guarantee sending him to Australia is not one of the options being considered."

"Well, just what are the options being considered?" my mother said. "Obviously something has to be done."

"I don't see that Albert has done anything so terribly wrong," Dad said.

"I agree that most of this trouble would never have happened if Jack Bannigore weren't such a fool," my mother said thoughtfully. "But the fact is that he is a fool, through and through, and so we're going to have to do something to stop this nonsense."

She paused and waited for my father to say something, but he didn't.

"I think the best thing," she finally said, "would be for Albert to sell his Zephyrcar and buy a moped or something. Something that Jack Bannigore won't object to."

"Sell it!" I howled. "Oh Mom! That's not fair."

"Who'd buy it?" Greta asked. "It doesn't even cut grass properly."

Dad set down his fork. "I don't know. That seems a bit extreme to me, too." He rubbed his chin. "You know, this whole problem may be taken out of our hands anyway, if the council passes that law banning Hovercraft in town. You'll have to get rid of it. You realize that, don't you?"

I nodded glumly. "Yes, I realize it. But maybe it won't pass."

"Maybe," he said. "How's this for a compromise? Let's wait and see what happens with that ordinance. If it passes, Albert has to sell his Zephyrcar. If it doesn't, we'll ask Sheriff Panziker to talk to Jack Bannigore about Albert. Okay?"

My mother gave it some thought. "Okay," she said after awhile, "on one condition. Albert can't use the Zephyrcar until they decide on that ordinance."

"Oh, no!" I groaned, burying my head in my hands.

"I'm tired of him being arrested every day. I'm beginning to feel like Ma Barker."

Dad looked at me and shrugged his shoulders. "Okay," he said. "That's the way it will be."

11

The Saturday of my mother's one-woman show arrived. She got up very early and was already dressed and pacing nervously when I got back from delivering my papers. I pulled off my soaking yellow rain poncho and came into the kitchen and sniffed and snuffled a few times to let her know how miserable I felt after delivering papers in the rain, on my ancient bike.

But she didn't notice my sniffles. In fact, she didn't notice me. She was too concerned about her show.

She had already chosen her paintings, but she seemed to be in the process of rechoosing everything.

"Maybe I should tighten the theme," she said to herself, "and just focus on my Tupperware studies."

She stewed around and fussed around. When my father got up, she asked him what he thought about her selection, and he told her everything was perfect.

"You couldn't have balanced the selection any better in a decade of deciding," he said. "This really shows the full range of—"

"The range!" she exclaimed. "I don't have any of my studies of ovens and griddles!" And with that she ran back into her studio.

My father looked at me and shrugged. "She's nervous," he said.

"Too bad it's raining so much," he added. "It'll cut down on the number of folks at the mall today. Let's go over later and cheer her on, okay?"

"Sure," I responded.

I went in and watched cartoons for a while. Wile E. Coyote was trying to catch the Roadrunner, but he kept getting smashed, scrunched, blown up, crushed, bombed, and otherwise thwarted. I had a lot of sympathy for the coyote.

Eventually, Mom and Greta left for the mall, and Dad left for the hardware store to buy furnace filters. I went on watching cartoons. I had just tuned into one about a talking dog that captured monsters when the words "News Flash" hit the screen.

Good grief, I thought, they started World War III and I didn't even get to use my Hovercraft again. What lousy luck!

But it wasn't World War III.

"The Ohio River has exceeded flood stage and is still rising," the voice said. "The Ohio River Authority predicts that the river will crest sometime next Tuesday at sixty-two feet. That would be the highest crest in more than twelve years. Residents in low-lying areas are advised to contact the local sheriff's office or fire station for information on evacuation procedures."

And then the cartoons resumed right in mid-battle. Tin Foil Dog was jamming himself into one of the monster's many cavities, causing the evildoer endless agony. Just as I was getting drowsy from so much animated action and adventure, another news bulletin flashed on.

This time it showed the inside of the Channel Six newsroom and one of their newscasters sitting at a desk.

"As we reported earlier," he said in the same ominous tones the other announcer had used, "the river has exceeded flood stage, and will be rising all weekend. We have the following live reports on flood-related problems in the Cincinnati area."

The picture switched to a street that was already under two or three feet of water. A reporter stood by the news van, talking about how many houses had been flooded and so on. As she talked, two women floated by in a rowboat.

The second scene shown looked familiar immediately, but it took me a minute to recognize it. Then I realized what it was. It was the Western Islands Shopping Mall. Only it looked like Lake Huron.

The reporter was on top of his van, and the water reached up to the headlights. "The floodwall collapsed here about twenty minutes ago," he was saying, "sending a virtual tidal wave rushing across the parking lot. Right now the water is three or four feet deep. But the dangerous factor is the current. It's coming through with such force that it literally swept a couple of cars away."

I'd been down to the mall dozens of times, and I could picture exactly what happened. The mall had been built right along the riverbank. The river ran along its entire southern edge and the city of Carlyle sort of wrapped around its other three sides. The architects had scooped the parking lot out so that it was several feet lower than the surrounding land, and then had built the mall on three islands of land that had been left at their regular height. The three islands were connected by fancy covered bridges with little ponds and gardens underneath them.

Apparently the retaining wall between the river and the parking lot had crumbled. And the result was an instant flood. The Western Islands Mall had literally become a trio of islands, surrounded by the waters of the Ohio River.

I watched the coverage for a few more minutes. Suddenly I noticed something in the background of the picture as the camera panned the scene.

"Hey!" I shouted. "That's my mom! And Greta! They're stuck on top of the bus!"

They were stranded right in the middle of the parking lot. Of course, so were dozens of other folks.

The reporter was saying, "The current is too swift for boats to navigate at this point. According to Carlyle's sheriff, Miller Panziker, the department has requested assistance from the county's helicopter rescue team, but the helicopter is currently being used elsewhere in the county."

"Hey, listen!" I shouted at the television set, "I could get in there and rescue them!" I pounded the arm of the couch. "I could fly in on the Zephyrcar."

I thought about it for a minute. I had to admit it looked a little dangerous. The water was moving pretty fast. But I had flown over that swimming pool without any trouble. Of course, I had been grounded from using the Zephyrcar. However, this was clearly an emergency.

While I was debating, the news reporter began to interview John Bannigore. I listened closely.

". . . and so the four-wheeled drive vehicles can't get in," he was saying. "The water covers their tail pipes and kills their engines. Plus the current's so swift that they're just about impossible to handle anyway."

"Well, Officer Bannigore, what is the next step?"

"Darned if I know," replied the officer.

That settled it for me. I knew what I had to do.

It was my civic responsibility!

I flew out of the garage, headed down Rose to Sixth, went down Sixth to Winfield, and started down Winfield to the Western Islands Mall. It was about three miles away. I figured I could be there in ten to fifteen minutes.

The first person I saw when I got to the mall was Baloney Jack Bannigore.

His eyes bulged. "You!" he sputtered. "You! How dare you come down here?" He was acting like the flood was my fault.

"I came to help," I said. "I can rescue people."

"Get out of here," he growled, "before I arrest you for interfering with police work!"

He didn't look like he was willing to discuss things any further, so I flew away.

On the other side of Baloney Jack was the Channel Six TV news van and a crowd of people. The news reporter was sitting on top of the van with his shoes and socks off and his pants rolled up above the knees. I hadn't noticed that when I'd seen him on TV.

In the opposite direction, where the parking lot curved around behind the mall, there were a few cars and some people and even a couple of boats. Around the edge of the parking lot was a five-foot ledge that had been left at ground level. Now it looked like the bank along a river.

Out across the water were dozens and dozens of cars, with people on top of about half of them. Near where the floodwall had broken away, a couple of cars had been overturned by the water. And close to the main entrance, about a hundred and fifty yards away, was my mother's VW bus. She and Greta were sitting on top of it, holding on to the paintings.

I would have gone straight out across the water to them, if it would have done any good. But it wouldn't have.

Not because the water was moving so fast. It was really ripping by, it's true, faster than I'd ever seen water go before. It reminded me of a water main break I'd seen on Vine Street in downtown Cincinnati once. The water had gushed out of a hole in the street at the top of a hill, and sluiced down in a bubbling rush that had knocked dogs, children, and small grown-ups off their feet. But that was nothing compared to this.

All the same, the current didn't scare me. I'd be six inches to a foot above it anyway.

The reason I didn't fly straight out to them was that I couldn't have helped them once I got there. Where would I have put a passenger? The Hovercraft couldn't fly with anybody much heavier than me in it. How would it fly with me and my mother? Or me and my sister? And what would they hang on to?

No, it wouldn't work. I could get out there to them, but I had to have some way of getting them back.

I flew along the edge of the rushing water. One of the cars parked on the bank looked familiar. As I drew closer, I recognized it: Bobby Herbert's old Galaxie. And there was Bobby, apparently trying to drown himself.

He was holding on to the sides of a flat-bottomed aluminum rowboat. After bracing himself in the rushing water, he leaped out of the water, flopped in mid-air like a carp, and smacked into the boat. Then, before he could grab the paddle and start stroking, the boat flipped over and threw him out. He spent a few minutes gathering underwater observations of the Western Islands Mall parking lot, and then bobbed spluttering to the surface. The boat floated over and clunked him in the back of the head. He grabbed the rope he'd tied to the bow of the boat and started fighting the current back toward the edge of the lot.

"Bobby!" I hollered.

He didn't hear me because of the roar of the water in the lot and the amount of water in his ears.

"Bobby!" I screamed even louder. This time he heard me.

"You!" he said, gagging. "What are you doing here? Especially with that thing!"

I had the feeling Officer Bannigore was writing his lines, but I ignored it.

"I'm here to help rescue people," I said.

Suddenly he looked wild. "Greta!" he moaned. "I've got to save Greta!" And with that he turned around and went through his entire drowning routine again.

When he reappeared, about ten feet farther down the lot, choking and spitting, I shouted at him, "I'm sure she finds your act very funny, but I don't see how it's going to help her any. And don't forget that my mother's out there, too. Okay?"

He looked at me hopelessly and gurgled.

"Listen," I said, "you'll never buck that current. It's too strong. But I can fly over it. Give me the boat and I'll go out and get them."

His expression changed to something between disbelief and disgust, like I had just proposed he swallow a handful of spiders. Finally he said, "Give you the boat? Are you crazy? This is my dad's fishing boat and I'm going to save Greta with it."

"I don't want it for keeps, Bobby! And you're not doing much of a rescue job with it!"

"Well, you couldn't do any better!" he screamed.

I didn't answer. I just gave the steering rod a pull and floated out over the water, making a wide loop around him and his boat, and going back over dry land.

He thought for a moment and then shouted, "Here. Catch."

He tossed the end of the rope to me. It made a wet slap against the side of the Zephyrcar. I bent over and grabbed it, said thanks, and started toward Mom and Greta out there on top of the VW bus.

But the dumb boat wouldn't cooperate. As I tugged it toward the bus, the current slammed into the side of the boat and whipped it right around behind me. That pulled the rope taut and suddenly the Zephyrcar began leaning to the left. I wasn't worried about tipping over, but I was worried about steering. The Zephyrcar was veering way off course because of the drag of the boat. It was heading straight for a light pole sticking up out of the water like a tree.

I had to do something. Fast.

I flew back to the edge of the water.

Bobby was just standing there watching me.

"Get in the boat!" I yelled.

"Why?" he asked.

"Just get in the boat! I need dead weight for ballast, and you'll do. And you can use the paddle a little to fight the current. Now get in!"

Bobby did a belly flop into the water, swam a struggling crawl forward about ten feet, and scrambled into the boat without tipping it over. While I edged forward he paddled around with his hands, and then with the short oar, until finally he had straightened out the boat behind my Zephyrcar.

"Albert," he hollered, "that thing you're flying. It won't blow up or anything will it?"

"How should I know, Bobby?" I called back over my

shoulder. I was feeling mean, and I wanted to keep him cooperative, so I added, "But what do you care? You're out to rescue Greta, aren't you?"

"Greta!" he whimpered, suddenly paddling ferociously. "Greta! I'm coming!"

"That's it, lover-boy," I murmured, "just keep that boat on course."

I leaned a little more on the stick and we picked up speed. Soon we were zipping over the water as though it were asphalt, and in no more than three minutes we were circling the VW bus.

"Albert!" my mother screamed. "I've never been so glad to see anybody!"

"Bobby!" Greta screamed. "I've never been so glad to see anybody!"

"We're both glad to see you guys," I said. "How are you doing?"

"All right, but we weren't looking forward to spending the night here," Mom said.

"Well, look, I think we can get you out without too much trouble. Mom, I think you'd better go first. We'll get the boat alongside the bus, and you slide down into it. Okay? Bobby'll help you."

I maneuvered the Zephyrcar around and Bobby did a pretty fair job of paddling, until we had the boat flush against the driver's side of the bus. My mother lay down on her stomach, feet first, her legs dangling down to the boat. She was just about to drop in when she suddenly stopped.

"Wait!" she cried. "I need to take my paintings! I can't leave them here. They'll be ruined."

"Hand them down, Mrs. Halperin," Bobby called. "We can take them in the boat."

So my mother handed him about fifteen of the paintings, and Bobby put them in the bow of the boat. Then she draped herself over the roof of the bus again, and climbed down into the boat, too. It bobbed dangerously for a moment, then calmed.

"Greta, you'll have to wait for the next run," I said. "There's not enough power to pull all of you."

"Golly," she wailed. "Mom, do I have to . . ."

"Greta, please do what your brother tells you," Mom said. "They'll be back for you in a few minutes. Just be thankful Albert's here to help us. And try to keep the rest of those paintings dry."

"Yes, Mother," Greta said meekly.

We made it out of that parking lot and over to the dry ground in about five minutes. It took a bit longer because of the extra weight. And also because I took a slightly longer route going back. Just out of spite—I already told you I was feeling a bit mean—I aimed at a spot midway between the TV news van and Officer Bannigore. And believe me, they all saw me coming.

When we pulled in, Officer Bannigore came sprinting up.

"You little idiot!" he gasped. "I told you to get out of here! I'm going to run you in for this!"

He was snarling at me. I mean it. He was snarling at me like a savage dachshund. But as he reached for me, we were mobbed. First the TV news crew came rushing in with a portable camera and a microphone, shouting questions at me and Bannigore. "What is that thing?" "Why do you want to arrest him?" "He's a hero, isn't he?"

Next came my mother, wading ashore like General MacArthur. She charged up to Baloney Jack.

"You listen to me, Jack Bannigore," she said. "You will not—"

Baloney Jack opened his mouth to object, but he never got a chance.

"I repeat," she said firmly, "*you will not* bother Albert until he has gone back out there to my bus and saved Greta . . ."

"Greta!" Bobby burbled in the background.

". . . and the rest of my paintings. Do you understand me?"

He shrugged and said, "Well, he's in direct violation of . . ."

But at that point Mom fixed him with a withering glare. Believe me, he didn't have a chance. No mortal could have withstood it. She'd used it on me only a couple of times, but I'd never forgotten. It was like having your soul X-rayed.

Baloney Jack stopped in mid-sentence and just looked at her. Slowly he shut his mouth.

Meanwhile, fifteen or twenty people—strangers who had relatives marooned in the parking lot or inside the shopping center—clustered around us, shouting and yelling. They all seemed to think I was working for the police and they wanted Officer Bannigore to order me to rescue their friends or relatives next.

While he was trying to shout them down and explain that he had nothing to do with me, I left with Bobby paddling behind me. We went back across the parking lot again, retrieved the rest of the paintings and Greta, and started back. When we were halfway, I put the Zephyrcar in neutral and turned around.

I was feeling so good I felt absolutely wicked. So I said, "Greta?"

"What, Albert?" she asked. She sounded suspicious.

"Aren't you glad I used my money to buy a Zephyrcar?"

She looked away and snorted.

"I couldn't hear you, Greta," I said.

"Oh, come on, Albert," she said, "let's get going."

"Hmm. I'm not sure I remember how to get this thing out of idle," I remarked to nobody in particular.

"Greta," Bobby said, "tell him, you're glad."

"All right, all right, Albert, you rat. I'm glad you bought a Zephyrcar."

"And you're very, very glad that I'm your brother?"

"Yeah."

"Say it," I ordered.

"I'm very, very glad you're my brother, you pinhead."

"Okay," I said. "I thought that's how you felt. It's just nice to hear you say it once in awhile."

With that we finished our trip.

The group around Baloney Jack had grown larger and noisier. They were all demanding that he do something. From the look on his face I was pretty sure he would have preferred to slice meat right then rather than almost anything else.

A portly little man with a tuft of cottony hair around his head stepped away from the crowd and approached me.

"Young man," he said in a surprisingly big voice, "do you see that blue Mercedes with an elderly woman on its roof?"

I looked in the direction he was pointing and saw—Mrs. Morgeld!

"Yes, sir," I said.

He reached into his back pocket, extracted a thick wallet, pulled a twenty-dollar bill from it, and handed it to me.

I stared at the bill with goggle eyes.

"That's yours for rescuing that woman, my wife," he said.

What a temptation that money was. But I couldn't help thinking about the look on poor—well, that's probably not the right word—on pitiful Mrs. Morgeld's face when the mud flew all over her. So I turned his money down.

"I'll get her, sir. But you won't owe me anything for it."

And I did get her, although for a moment, when she slid down the side of her car into the boat, I thought we were going to lose her. The boat rocked violently and nearly tipped her out.

After I brought her back safely, everybody began clamoring for my help. Some of them were waving cash at me, and one man hollered, "Will you accept a check?" But I didn't feel right about charging them, either. So I did the best I could to sort through all of their demands and pleas. I went after people who were stuck in the most dangerous spots first, and the people with small children. I even rescued three dogs and a cat from cars that were on the verge of submerging. Eventually I got them all. Bobby wore out after about forty minutes, but there were plenty of volunteers to help me by paddling the boat. And when I began to worry about gas, somebody dashed off and brought back a full two-gallon can for me.

I ended up having a mighty long afternoon at the shopping mall, but when it was all over with, I had to admit I rather enjoyed it.

12

The river eventually went down, of course. Late Tuesday night it crested and by Friday it was low enough that they were able to tow the cars out of the Western Islands Mall parking lot. The break in the floodwall had been sandbagged, and it was permanently repaired a couple of weeks later. After a while the excitement died down and things returned to normal.

But for a couple of days my Zephyrcar and I were the talk of Cincinnati, not to mention Carlyle.

We were on Channel Six news, and the other two local stations got there later in the day. And we made the front page of the daily paper—the very paper I delivered. They made quite a big deal out of the fact that I was one of their delivery boys and that I used the Zephyrcar to make deliveries.

From then on the Zephyrcar and I were fixtures in Carlyle as we delivered papers each morning. The City Council never did take up that proposed ordinance to ban Hovercraft. As far as I know, it was just dropped.

About a week after the flood I received a phone call from the manager of Western Islands Mall. She was very complimentary and said how appreciative the mall was that I helped rescue people who were stranded by the flood. "My pleasure," I said. And then she said, "That's nice, but we'd like to give you a token of our appreciation." The mall merchants had each kicked in a contribution and they wanted to give it to me at a small ceremony at the mayor's office.

"My pleasure," I said again. And then I asked, "Uh, how much is that token?"

"Five hundred dollars," she said.

I dropped the phone.

Now my ledger looked like this:

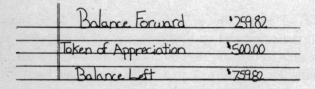

Balance Forward	$259.82
Token of Appreciation	$500.00
Balance Left	$759.82

The money was a big surprise. But perhaps even more surprising was the editorial that appeared in the *Hilltopper* that same week, which praised "the ingenuity and bravery of one of our young people, who rescued several people from the massive Western Islands Mall flood. This young man, who deserves our thanks and appreciation, is none other than Albert Halibut."

Oh well. You can't have everything.

At least Officer Bannigore left me alone after that. In fact, I hardly ever saw him. Once, when I was out delivering my papers, I saw him coming toward me, but he suddenly made a U-turn and sped away. Urgent police business, no doubt.

Mom's exhibition had to be moved because of water damage in the mall. She had her paintings shown at one of the downtown galleries, a fancy place near the Art Museum. We all went to the opening and stood around, sipping Coke

from plastic cups, and chit-chatting with the Morgelds and their friends for a couple of hours. I even had to wear a suit. But it was worth it. Mom said afterward she was so happy that her jaw got sore from smiling.

Things also got back to normal with Greta, more or less. She became her old gruesome self again.

In fact, things became so normal that it got boring.

And then, one day, I got a letter in the mail. From the Future Perfect Manufacturing Company.

I tore it open and read it eagerly. It said:

Dear Zephyrcar Owner:

With great pleasure we announce the development of a brand new product—the Future Perfect Gyrocopter! That's right! A personal, one-person helicopter that can be yours for only . . .

A smile spread across my face and my mind filled with visions. I knew that things weren't going to be boring much longer.